E. V. B.

A Garden of Pleasure

E. V. B.

A Garden of Pleasure

ISBN/EAN: 9783337070151

Printed in Europe, USA, Canada, Australia, Japan

Cover: Foto ©Andreas Hilbeck / pixelio.de

More available books at **www.hansebooks.com**

A GARDEN OF PLEASURE

A GARDEN OF PLEASURE

BY

E. V. Boyl

Author of ' Days and Hours in a Garden,'
' Ros Rosarum,' etc.

' Who loves a garden, still his Eden keeps.'

A. ALCOTT. 1799

LONDON

ELLIOT STOCK, 62 PATERNOSTER ROW, E.C.

1895

DEDICATED

TO MY ELDEST GRANDCHILD, CECIL
ALBINIA ARBUTHNOT, WHOSE DELIGHT
IS IN THE GARDEN, AND WHO MADE
IT THE EDEN OF HER CHILDHOOD.

CONTENTS

PREFACE

Since a preface is said to be a necessary evil, it may perhaps be utilised as a means for the embodying of a few notes on subjects not contained in the book itself. Among these, it should be explained that those flowers—wild or cultivated—whose outlines face first pages of the months, are not supposed to follow in any order of succession as to their proper flowering seasons. They were drawn solely for pure love of them, and were arranged wheresoever they seemed to suit the best.

On finally looking through the proof sheets, the writer has to confess to a disappointing sense of inadequacy; a pervading, uneasy impression of how poor a thing after all these slight garden records are. The flowers named in them so few—so scanty the attempted portrayal of

*them !   Most emphatically so, when I see the sun-bright
garden in all the joy and glory of this royal month of
May—now, with Nature at full flood and flow of Spring!
with the great elms in the background, half-drest in a fairy
garment of budding green.   The severity and fatal length
of the long winter endured in the garden—though many
a tender shrub and plant has died of it—is forgotten in a
moment ; and indeed it seems on the whole almost to have
inspired fresh life and vigour of growth in those delicious
things which we call Spring flowers.   The rich abundance of
our early favourites this year is undiminished.   Though
long in coming, now that they are here at last they seem
more brilliantly beautiful than ever.   If any long-loved
habitual pleasure of the garden fails to-day, it is that
birds are fewer.   There are fewer thrushes, and we
miss the rapture of their music.   Blackbirds must
know the secret of some less precarious means of living,
for* they *are as numerous as ever.   Yet somehow
Merula's magic note is, or so it seems to me, less wholly
dear than is the singing of the thrush.   The air he sings
is so brief, the burden of it so sad !   He only sings over*

and over, ' *Di Memoria nudrirsi, piu che di speme !* ' ' *I live on Memory more than hope.*' Of course he does not mean it in the least ! but so the tune wears on in sad, sweet, iteration. In the winter, after Christmas, the holly trees in the garden shone scarlet, loaded as they were with berries. We had planned to cut away several branches of them, but until the birds had stript the fruit, the gardener's knife was not to be lifted for the pruning. Yet scarcely had ' the wise thrush ' begun to feast, when down there swooped upon the hollies such flocks of field-fares from the open country that, in a day the trees were bare. So the poor throstles—to whom of right the garden fruits belong—starved and were found dead in numbers. The motto of wild Nature is always neces-sarily, ' *Live, and let die who may.*' And thus there is many a small tragedy enacted often, in the garden. One of the most pathetic perhaps, when a tiny mother-bird was found dead in a thorny brier, pierced to the heart by thorns in the Rose-Home of her choice.

At this very time, as I write, through the open window comes fitfully the complaint of a solitary dove *who sits all day alone in the great red horse-chestnut. His story is a sad one. On a cold March day, twelve months ago, a ring-dove appeared no one knows whence and timidly presented himself outside the garden porch. The bird was lame and hungry, and very shy; but after three weeks of persevering attention from us, he grew fat and tame, and came regularly to feed with the pigeons. Very soon he found a mate, and brought her also with him to feed. Then they made a nest in the red chestnut tree, and in due time the pair brought a fine young one to be admired and fed at the door. Then all three flew away to the woods. Again, last March, the Dove reappeared one day, and his mate was with him and the young one too. But they only stayed a day, and never returned. And now the widowed dove sits all day in the chestnut tree, and calls and calls. From early morning till late afternoon the plaintive cry is heard: the poor bird is forsaken, and it is plain that life for him has lost its interest. Another song comes now and again from far off among the leaves; and as I listen to* the unutterable sweetness of that sylvan note, the old long-remembered lines recur and keep time with the wood-pigeon's music.

> ' I heard a stock-dove sing or say
> His homely tale this very day;
> His voice was buried among trees
> Yet to be come at by the breeze:
> He did not cease, but cooed, and cooed;
> And somewhat pensively he wooed.
> He sang of love with quiet blending,
> Slow to begin and never ending,
> Of serious faith and inward glee,
> That was the song—the song for me.' *

Heavily has the great frost told on evergreens in the garden. The yew hedges which are our pride, look thin and seared. There is scarce a berberis left alive, and we shall sorely miss those exquisite carpets of yellow and orange which summer by summer did use to spread beneath the shrubs when their little gold bells drop; and there will be no berries ripening in purple bloom. And lavender, on which we set such store, has also suffered, so that the harvest of its fragrant yield will be less rich this year than ever we remember.

* Wordsworth.

Yet counting all the change and loss that the passing of the seasons has brought, since those other ' Days and Hours in a Garden' of more than ten years ago— enough remains of beauty and delight for us to feel joyously as ever, the 'ver perpetuum' that irradiates the garden—whether it be small or great—the Garden that we call our own. Of that beloved spot well may it be said,

> ' An hour with thee !—when earliest day
> Dapples with gold the eastern grey,
> Oh, what can frame my mind to bear
> The toil and tumult, cark and care,
> New griefs, which coming hours unfold,
> And sad remembrance of the old ?
>   One hour with thee !

> ' One hour with thee !—When sun is set,
> Oh, what can teach me to forget
> The thankless labours of the day,
> The hopes and wishes flung away ;
> .   .   .   .
>   One hour with thee !' *

Lovers of their garden should have that feeling for it strong within them, or their love cannot be true.

And now, departing not from the custom which holds

* Sir Walter Scott.

with letters as with prefaces, and by which the last word is wont to be the most important, a word must be said for the Chief Toiler of the garden, in whose hands lies the responsibility of success or failure. Perhaps there may not be many who would choose a gardener on such lines as these : not many would, so to speak, take the candidate into the garden, and pointing to a cabbage or a currant bush, give the order thus—'Dig a hole and plant that currant head downwards' ; and if forthwith the man did as he was told without a word, engage him on the spot! Yet I believe such imperiousness does exist, and then, is fatal to the garden. We may love dearly our flowers; we may know (or think we know), everything about them, and call them all by their names. We may believe we are Master, and that things being done entirely under our own directions everything will grow, and all will be well. Yet nevertheless nothing will grow, nothing will be well unless the gardener is also in a sense, on his side, master. When his worth is ascertained, give him a free hand over all affairs which come specially under his control.

Give him a living interest in the garden by letting him exercise his taste (subject always to yours), in planting and in arrangement of colours, etc., and by showing your own constant interest in it ; and if the man be possessed of good Intelligence and Experience, if his heart is in his work, if he has it in him to Succeed, succeed he will. The garden and the gardener will grow as it were, to understand one another, and you to trust and understand them both, while your content and gladness in the garden will increase and grow with the year's increase.

And here a grateful tribute must find place, for the Gardener, JESSE FOULK, by whose rare skill this plot grew into a Garden of Pleasure, whose ceaseless care has maintained its charm for three-and-twenty summers, and who completes the Thirtieth year of his devoted service on the 22nd of May: with which well-omened date I close my Preface.

ELEANOR VERE BOYLE.

HUNTERCOMBE MANOR,
May, 1895.

JANUARY

A

JANUARY

' Life is a road, at either end a gate,
  The gate of Life behind—of Death beyond.
 Love guards the path and guides us all the way,
   As through a garden where calm Hope doth rest.'
                                    G. F. Bodley.

JANUARY 1894.—At last the white snow
sheet is lifted, and we draw a breath
of relief as it were, after the tension of a
long long winter. It was not really long,
however, it only lasted about three weeks
or so. And there have been brilliant sun-
shines, and early morning splendours were
not rare, when the lawns became wide
diamond-fields, as pure and sparkling as
winter's frost could freeze them. Splendours also there have been, of sunset skies
whose glory died not until the utmost
remotest glow of green had faded into
grey. Wondrous joys such as these are,

must be now foregone ; for they perforce
have waned with the frosty nights, and
scarcely a regret goes with them, so happy
is the feeling of the warmer air, and the
smell of the grass set free at last from the
ice-king's iron grip. Instantly, upon his
departure, little sharp blades of crocus,
with the broader pale green shafts of
daffodil have arisen inches above ground,
and ' daisies, pearled Arcturi of the earth,'
will soon be born among the grass. Even
in the gentian border there appears one
poor bell of pinched and sickly blue,
gleaming faintly among its frost-tainted
leaves.

The first anxious visit after such severity
of frost, is of course paid to the little
clump of Olearia, near the western end of
the rockery. A dozen or so of plants
were grown from tiny cuttings, sent from
the Isle of Wight, two years and a half ago.
After most tender nursing they grew into
fine young plants, as large as an ordinary
lavender bush of the same age, and were
duly planted out. Last summer they were
literally white all over with little daisy

flowers. In the autumn (at the time that they were sheltered carefully under thick green spruce branches), each little spray and twig was loaded with a mass of buds just formed.

Alas! a glance underneath the covering at once betrayed the irremediable hurts our pets had suffered. They were all brown and grey, diffusing a sort of sickly fragrance, not perceptible in their summers of full strength and inflorescence. It has to be confessed, that our garden lies too low, and is not sufficiently dry, to suit some things.

Gentians seem to be always blowing : the vitality of them is marvellous; there was one on a patch niched snugly in the rock garden, that bloomed on for ever! It displayed its ultramarine magnificence every day for fully six weeks. Every day when the sun shone, I did homage to it. Sometimes the blue of it was so velvety, so brilliant, that one could scarce forbear to stoop and kiss its open face! I find this in my garden diary : 'Oct. 15. A large blue gentian on Roman walk. It

shuts up when very cold, and opens wide
in the sun at noon.' 'Nov. 18. The Gentian there still.'   On Nov. 27, 'Poor little
gentian has begun to fade;' and then,
Dec. 1, 'The Gentian is withered away.'
It grew on a glossy-leaved, vigorous root,
sheltered by a flat stone ledge, in a pocket
half way up the bank, facing due south.
This strange flower, with its movements of
opening and closing, and its colour-changes
of expression, resembled almost some live
sea-creature.   In May the plant is sure
to bloom again, between great cushions
of pink and snowy phlox Nelsonii. But
then, its natural life will not last for more
than a week or two.

It is like a 'far-off melody,' to return in
thought from the grand deep azure gentian
of the mountain-side or the garden, to its
little sister of our own wild English heaths.
It was near the sea coast where first we
met, on one of the loveliest of miniature
moors, where a sudden hollow hides the
unsightly crowd of surrounding villas. The
September sun shone down in softened
brilliance, and the blowing breeze put one

in mind of Scotland. The brown heath-
land glowed with autumn-flowering furze;
that low creeping kind which inter-threads
among the heather, and glows in the sunshine like embroidery of the richest gold.
There remained still some scattered tufts
of pink bell-heather and ling ; green-grey
lichen at their roots, variegated with
delicious tones the all-prevailing brown.

Suddenly, low among the moss, in a wet
boggy spot, between two heathery fir-
crowned braes, I became aware of a soft
gleam of blue. It was the pale azure of
wild gentian. The flowers were opened
wide in all their gentle loveliness, drinking
in the full joy of mid-day.

It may not be rare, I believe it to be only
what is called 'local,' but to me it was
absolutely new. It is very delicate and
shy—and how exquisite is its dream-like
reflex of that other deep blue dweller on
the Alps! The place where it grew was
still, as might be any moorland solitude
miles away from everybody. Only an in-
distinct low murmur either of the sea or
noises of the town, mingled with light

whisperings among the pine tops, floated
through the air around. Above the olive-
green and tawny sedges where these earth
stars shone, each one single and alone
on its short upright stalk, there came
an Atalanta butterfly leisurely wandering
across the valley. . . . I hope it was not
a very brutal impulse that moved me to nip
off and gather into a little bunch every
one of those wild Gentian flowers, and take
them carefully away! Some covetous eye
was almost sure to spy them out, some
heedless hand would pull up the roots and
carry them away to perish. But it seemed
rather like doing evil that good might
come !

More than nine years have slipped
by since the last of these garden notes in
September 1883. A new series was begun
in the February following, breaking off
before November. Three months are now
worked in to complete the twelve. Through
all these days and hours, changes of every
kind have passed over the old Bucking-
hamshire garden. Nine times has Spring
bloomed and ripened into summer there.

Summer suns have burned and failed ; Autumn leaves have fallen in showers of rustling gold, and winter·winds have swept them away. Old trees are gone and new trees have been planted, and everywhere about the place reigns the inevitable law of change. Old paths have been turned, flower-beds here and there have been turfed over, or new ones made. Yet now things seem as if they ought always to have been just so, and no other way at all! A new sundial, put together with old carved stones and cement, now stands upon the east lawn between the Sequoia gigantea, and the Cedar. Already it wears the look of having stood there for years. There is a motto worked upon the steps in Latin : it means, ' Light and shade in turn, but Love always.' Round the top, just below the dial, three lions walk with solemn step from the sun-rising southward, towards the east again.

The chiefest change of all, is the creation of Peach Corner. On the sunny side of a very old brick wall which had probably formed the boundary between the garden

and the stable yard in former days, lay a
rubbishy square plot of ground.   Here
were summered out the Camellias and
Azaleas etc., etc.   Here also was the place
of dilapidated frames, and all sorts of orra*
plants, and empty flower-pots.   Old Peach
trees were trained on the wall, and we used
to think that peaches reddened riper there
than on other walls.   But the Peach trees
kept on decaying year by year, making
less hard the decision to remove them.
When the time came for destroying the
bit of old brick work—that was a harder
matter ; not undertaken until after endless
hesitations, yet not regretted since.   The
walk on the north side used to end in
gloomy shade under a very large old
Phylleria, growing in a narrow border full
of melancholy ferns.   Now, a much-needed
thoroughfare is gained by carrying on the
walk beyond.   The great Phylleria breathes
freer now, rejoicing in the sun which, for
the first time warms its rugged old grey
stem.   Excepting upon its umbrageous

* 'Orra,' a Scotch word used for anything laid
anywhere out of the way.

upper half, above the wall, this tree had
never seen the sun since George Evelyn
planted the row of Phyllereas, in imitation
apparently of that at his cousin's place at
Wotton.

Smooth bare poles alone remain of all the
others : yet such is their vitality, although
to ·all appearance they have long been
dead, that from the roots have sprung
a thicket of young wood, so luxuriant
as almost to hide the barren decay of
the parent stems. Since Peach Corner
commended itself as a pleasant name for
the new 'improvement,' after the place
was cleared fresh soil filled in and the
walk extended—to justify the title three
double blossomed standard peach trees,
are placed there in the grass. In the
remnant of old wall, arched openings have
been worked with a lattice of thin wire
strained across, up which Mina lobata
climbed joyously last summer to the very
top, and then fell over, breaking in a
rich mantling of leaf, light and lovely as
folds of green lace might be. When mina
lobata starts to grow, about the middle or

end of August, nobody else can possibly climb so fast.   Her flower is of no account ; but it no more is needed than the leaves to which belong so much of grace and charm.   In a sunny angle of Peach Corner, there is a William Richardson rose.   Beautiful as it is, it comes not near, nor never will, to the wonder of one that grew in the gardens of La Mortola, nearly twenty feet high, and crowned with hundreds of orange-hearted roses.   The rose called, 'Idèale,' delights and disappoints by turns in the opposite corner.   In the border near them, flourished in the later days of summer, a strange black dahlia.

It is altogether unlike its name, and yet dahlia it is most certainly, by the leaves and the stiff long stalk, by the bud and the flower and the root.   At first sight, you would say it was a potentilla of unusual size.   For a *dahlia*, it is very small indeed ; and the velvet-black of it never fails to charm, whether growing in the open border or mixed in when cut, with very bright late-blooming flowers.   In late summer

days, Peach Corner is crowded with delicious things; there is yellow Cassia,
luxuriantly gay throughout the day, and
after sunset so forlorn with drooping leaves
shut close together like the sensitive plant.

Nicotiana, whose dejection lasts all the
while that Cassia has her day, but who
breaks forth in white shining stars at dusk,
cobalt Comelina and sweet verbena and
apple-scented salvia dotted over with a
tiny scarlet flower, and pale blue daisies.
There is an edging of Sea-Pink or Thrift.
(Why is it Thrift? Is it because it thrives
everywhere, in the richest or the poorest
soil?) In another part of the garden there
is a strip of a variety that glows with a
deeper tone of pink. These came from a
garden in the Highlands, where the sunny
middle walk, edged with Sea-Pink, led up
to an arbour, overgrown with convolvulus
and white honeysuckle, and surrounded by
sweet peas. No one ever sits in an arbour
now-a-days. I think they are never made
now, and dear old Mrs Sherwood's story in
that delicious fifty years' ago penny series
of hers (tiny little books in various coloured

paper covers), entitled 'The Lady in the Arbour,' could not have been written now. In the woodcut frontispiece, the lady, drest in a scanty short-waisted gown, a cap on her head, and a narrow shawl pinned round her shoulders, sits in the arbour with a book on her knee. It is a prim, precise looking latticed arbour, with no wild garlanding of anything about it. Behind is a bit of old broken park paling, and a very black wood. Through a gap in the paling creeps a little child, as if intent on making its way to the lady in the arbour. I think the idea was, that the lady waited there every morning for the wood-cutter's child to read to it from the Bible on her lap. Not much, perhaps, in the simple little story to interest a child-reader. The charm must have lain in that picture of the gap, with its infinite suggestions of all that might lie beyond the wood, and of all there might be on the other side, of moss or snail-shells, or velvety field mouse among the withered leaves and sticks.

What would I not give to see again

those little penny books with their Bewick-
like woodcuts! Alas! I seek them in vain.
I can recall a few titles such as 'The
Rosebuds,' 'The Little Dog Flora, and
her Silver Bell,' 'The Two Dolls,' 'The
Snow,' 'Sophronia and her Kitten.' Very
little hope remains of copies of these or any
others ever rewarding my long search. But
we have wandered far from Peach Corner.
Through the glass walls of the green-house
which bounds one side, come gleams of
scarlet geranium and of red winter carnations. The raised border alongside is
this year filled with double violets. They
are the dark purple kind that are never
met with now. Their scent is powerful;
and if a drawback to their cultivation
exists, it is only that their stalks are too
short. Aubretia hangs over the stone
edges of this violet bed, and we half-per-
ceive behind the glass, a grove of arum
lillies, with all the promise of their long
spirals soon to untwist and open out in
broad patches of ivory white.

The great Rhynchospermum jasminoides,
which for years had filled up one corner

of the house is dead. Early summer used to clothe it in white waxen clusters, for our delight. Both the old and the new aubretias are here ; the new grows the strongest, but the colour of it is too much mixt with red to please so greatly as the old. When the common aubretia begins to show in lilac upon its compact mass of grey-green cushion, the image of a never-forgotten April evening at Farringford fails not to return to me, with all the freshness of a dearly cherished memory.

The straight garden path sloped gently upwards to an open summer-house, where sat the Poet Laureate, discoursing with his friends.

It was the season when aubretia shone in all the bloom of her lilac loveliness, up and down the borders. Later on, white lilies would rise in tall groups at the back. In the trees all around, thrushes and blackbirds were celebrating the early spring at the top of their voices. The hour was late, and efforts were ineffectually made to persuade him to return to the house.

But the air was so balmy, and he was so happy sitting there, in the garden, enjoying the soft glow of evening light,—that go into the house he would not. Presently however, as he saw the sky grow grey and misty, wiser counsels prevailed, and then he rose and left the garden. As we slowly wended to the house along the deeply shadowed path between the trees, he pointed to some bushes of the small leaved laurel growing amongst the others. They were his favourites he said : the Victor's Laurel of ancient Greece, and he told of how they loved the shade, and grew the best underneath thick trees.

Well is it for us that no voice whispers to the heart, sometimes when we say farewell, 'It is the last time, nevermore.' It was the last time I ever saw the beloved poet ; a few months passed by, and then the world was poorer by the loss of him who had been given to live so long his noble poet's life amongst us, 'unhasting, unresting like a star ;' a star that shines forever now, in 'heaven's clear calm.'

Outside the greenhouse door, a small

B

patch of Guernsey lilies grow and thrive. When I am absent at the time of their flowering, a box containing one or two blooms, most beautifully pink, is sure to reach me wherever I may be. In the small Propagating House near by, Dendrobium nobilis is richly flowering. I believe this dendrobium to be the oldest variety known in England, and our plant has flourished with us for well nigh forty years, having accompanied us from the old Somerset home. Beside it in delicious contrast, are many clusters of amber-fringed D. fimbriata. The vitality of Nobilis is so strong, that the flower will survive without water, or even worn as a ' button-hole ' for almost the whole length of a day. There is an interesting young tree in a small pot in this house, an infant Dragon Tree. It is a seedling from Tenerife, where, till lately, lived that ancient Dragon, recorded to have seen at least two thousand years. They tell me that in about a century, our specimen may have attained the height of four feet. Where shall all we be then ? The most interesting inhabitant of this

'Touch us gently, Time !
We've not proud nor soaring wings
Our ambition, *our* content
Lies in simple things,
Humble voyagers are We,
O'er life's dim unsounded sea,
Seeking only some calm clime :—
Touch us gently, Time !'—*Barry Cornwall.*

house, however, is a large Eft. I found him one day outside the door, in a puddle of rain, asking, as plain as words, to be allowed to get inside to be warm. So I took the clammy creature up, and placed him within amongst the ferns and pebbles, and never since has he vouchsafed us a single glimpse of himself. This is a draw-back, for he is extremely handsome. Black, with orange spots, and orange throat. Efts of this kind are not uncommon, though, perhaps, seldom seen so large as our friend, who measured something like ten inches. They are found under stones in dampish places, mostly in churchyards. The small dry brown efts, that sometimes walk in at the door from the garden, are not so handsome, but certainly are pleasanter to handle, and the expression of their face is rather pathetic.

Once, and once only, in the far past, I found a Golden Eft! It must have been the Queen eft, and it dwelt in one of the most fascinating ponds on Wimbledon Common. The colour was purest yellow-gold, and near its head it wore beautiful crested gills. There exists a curious and almost universal ignorance about these our lowly fellow-creatures; about all 'reptiles' indeed.

A boy who had 'finished his education' at school, invited us the other day to come and look at a leech. The 'leech' turned out to be an eft (or as the country people say, an 'effet'). Long ago, snakes abounded in the garden at certain seasons of the year. They were most harmless snakes, but never are they seen now, so determined has been the enmity against them, so constantly have they been destroyed whenever silly enough to let themselves be seen. Once, I met a beauty four feet long, gliding through the half open orchard gate, into the stable yard. And in those days, I dreamed a dream one night of a great snake-fight raging in the path near the hedge in the House meadow. Next morning the dream was verified, for walking along that path, on the very spot where the visionary fight took place, I came upon the broken up bodies and bones of three snakes. They must have been destroyed by some one with a stick who had caught them unawares while in the blind fury of deadly combat. I think these beautiful creatures are scarcer everywhere than in former days. It is very long since I have rejoiced at the sight of a snake in some wild place, slipping through the long green grass—'a beauteous wreath with melancholy eyes '—or undulating across a streamlet.

Harmless and graceful however as is the common snake, an adder is quite a different affair! No living creature bears a more sinister expression. The form of the small cruel head, and the faultlessly regular and even chain-pattern along the back. The very shade of cold pale brown that colours it, and the glassy green of its under side, seem to bear a wicked look. One may well fear 'a snake in the grass' of *that* species! In the garden, animated Nature is always as full of charm, (at least to me!) as are the flowers. A pair of small call-ducks wander here at will. Sir Francis, the drake, is very handsome : plumaged like a mallard. His partner takes

not the slightest notice of him. She quite
ignores his devotion, though he follows her
about continually, and scarcely eats himself,
till she has had her fill. One peculiarity
is, that they are essentially dry ducks.
They have a holy horror of water—the
pond in the field which one would suppose
might be such a comfort in hot weather,
they carefully avoid. When it rains, they
waddle inside the porch. And when the
walks and grass happen to be wet, they are
quite uncomfortable, and scramble up on
to any dry place they can find, to be out of
the damp. On the other hand, these ducks
will make believe to wash on the very
dryest gravel, and will clap their wings
and dip as if the gravel were deep waters!
Some very secret inhabitants of the garden
are the hedgehogs; they are scarcely ever
seen but on · one day in the year. On
warm June evenings, I begin to watch for
the old mother hedgehog, who never fails
to bring out her young family (almost invariably three) for their first survey of the
wide wide world of green turf, under the
elms, at the northern end of the garden.

The chosen spot is very solitary and far removed, and rarely does the old one permit us to catch the least glimpse of her prickles! But the three little ones are not so wary. It is very nice to take one of them in one's hand, and peer into the little black face and deep-set sparkling eyes, and feel the soft under-fur and the little cool feet! One evening however, (there were but two that summer) the young ones rolled up instantly upon hearing footsteps: and although a watch was kept at a distance for full twenty minutes, the little prickleys never moved. So we left them to themselves.

All winter through, up to the end of March, or longer, cocoa-nuts hang from the Rose Arches for the titmice. The hole is always made in the lower part, so as to discourage the sparrows, who do not fancy hanging head downwards. (It is not that they couldn't do it, for there is nothing they cannot do if they try!) For a long time they did not understand that cocoa-nut was good. But unfortunately a nut-hatch let fall some crumbs of it one day:

and then the sparrows found out how nice
it was. At regular intervals in the short
winter days, the titmice come to feed—
about four of each kind. There is the
great tomtit, masterful and quarrelsome.
The cole-tit, very brisk and persevering;
the little blue-cap, most lovely and timid
and yielding in its ways, and that other tit
which is almost the cole-tit with a differ-
ence. It may be the male cole, or it may
be the Nun. It was on a morning in last
June that a mother cole-tit—tiny and
fascinating little mite !—brought out her
newly flown brood to introduce them
to me and the cocoa-nuts. I watched
from the oak-room window, which exactly
faces the line of rose arches. The little
mother pecked out little beakfuls of nut,
darting to and fro with flits and flirts of
wings and tail, feeding the young, and
trying to teach them how to get at the
food for themselves. After a time they
all flew ; and for several minutes the side
of the yew hedge was alive with minute
tits climbing and clinging all over it.
Then they got back to the nuts, and one

tiny creature in a futile way tried to imitate its parent. But hanging topsy-turvy is rather an impossible trick for a beginner, so it didn't try any more, but set to work at the green-fly on the rose-shoots. The young tit family did not appear again, but a nut-hatch brought her one chick for several mornings to the rose arches.

It was nearly as big as its mother, and seemed all head and shoulders. It sat shivering and fluttering, while she dug at the nut, every few moments extracting a morsel, and stuffing it down the chick's throat. It did not attempt to dig for itself; when it flew off, one saw how strong on the wing it was. When the nut is fresh, shreds fly about as the nut-hatch hacks it, and then the birds become quite playful; dashing after the flying fragments and catching them in the air before they fall.

FEBRUARY

II

FEBRUARY, 1884

'Gloomy winter's now awa'.'

SUDDENLY, without any warning as it were, winter is away. There's a new sound in the air, 'a new face at the door.' This is Sunday and the sound is the rooks' consultation in the tops of the great Elms (they always arrange matters on a Sunday), while in the garden, the air seems full of the voices of birds. Through the budding branches and the thickness of the winter greens is woven a network of melody, where a thousand little finches twitter, and blackbirds and thrushes just lightly touch their long silent notes. And there's a vision of the sweetest face in all the world—the first pale glimpse of Spring with her snowdrop crown. It was but yesterday the Snowdrops had

scarce begun to show in silvery points above
the earth—to-day the slender stalks have
risen two inches high! There are pure
white double primroses and a few coloured,
in every part of the garden, where so late
as yesterday there seemed to be none.
Even the yellow of a winter aconite, or
the blue of scyllas, begin to show here
and there. I do not know if the sap does
actually rise at the touch of spring, but
there has come a fresher green in the
broad blue-green iris leaves, and the ends
of the long rose sprays are flushed with
emerald, and a warmer green glows through
the prickly junipers. This first awaken-
ing comes rather later than usual. Though
the season has been so mild, it was unusually dark, and in my garden diary for
December I find fifteen days marked 'very
dark.' In January there were indeed days
when we beheld the sun, but it has been
mostly a reign of darkness, and earth's
stars, which are the flowers, are few.

These Snowdrops! year after year they
come again to test our appreciation of form
and simplicity, and every year their

triumph is assured. I challenge you to show me the grandest bell-flower born of tropic suns that can compare in its attributes of perfect grace with our English snowdrop. I mean the large old single snowdrop—I will have nothing to do with the double, as a snowdrop. The snowdrop is in itself a lesson of form and colour— from the straight, long oval of the tube, out of which spring three sweet oval lobes, to the delicate pencilling in Nature's loveliest green of the threefold inner cup. And you will observe there is no over-luxuriant fulness, all is severely, tenderly restrained, as are the lines of a Greek statue. And then the colour! it is pure as fresh-fallen snow upon an alpine peak. The hanging of the bell, too, is a wonder of firm lightness, so light that with a breath it swings, so strong it will upbear the snow-drift. One lovely detail must not be forgotten : this is the folding inwards of the lobes along each outer edge, giving a peculiar grace which hard lines here could never have. But an attempt to describe the snowdrop must fail; I know of no words simple

enough, nor any language rich enough to
give its perfect beauty. Dear innocent
flower of home! There are exiles under
skies of eastern drouth whose brave hearts
faint with longing if they do but for a
moment dwell upon the thought of your
cold loveliness.

FEBRUARY 14.—The happy birds are
keeping St Valentine's Day, and I have
found an Echo! There seems ever a
weird charm in the mysterious presence
which makes such arbitrary choice of some
special spot, building or rock, and lives
there for ever silent and unknown until
awoke by chance, and then is so warily on
the watch, ever ready to start up and mock
the passer-by with a hollow imitation of
his voice or footstep. Doubtless there is
some scientific explanation, but it does
really seem that Echo is a capricious being,
and will come and go much as she pleases;
else why is it that, after haunting a place
for years, she will sometimes disappear one
day without rhyme or reason, and never
come back? I have not thought of it for

C

many a year; but at this moment I remember like yesterday a lovely echo, or
group of echoes, somewhere in Switzerland, I think it was on the Grindelwald,
within view of the Great Scheideck. A
man played a little tune on an immense
shepherd's horn. The travellers listened
and after a pause Echo gave back the air
note for note with clear and sweet preci-
sion; and then from hill to hill her hermit
sisters took up the music over and over
again till the sounds became small and far,
dying away in a fairy-like *diminuendo*.
That is how memory recalls to me the
beautiful Fairy of the Scheideck Pass. But
our new-comer dwells somewhere near the
end of a brick wall partly covered with
ivy. She, too, is a fairy, but of coarser
mould, and she can only repeat once. I
was startled by the sudden mockery early
one morning as I called my dog, and I can
solemnly affirm that this Echo has only
just arrived and settled in the wall; for
close by, it is an almost daily occurrence to
turn and call the dog in, before shutting
the garden gate and we have never before

heard her voice. Echoes are rare here on the flat. We had one in a gable of the house, but she went away or was lost when the yew hedges were planted. In some counties they say the bulls in the fields are made savage by hearing their own cries re - echoing from the woods and hills around.

We have had busy days of late trimming the creepers all round the house. Long prunings of honeysuckles and jasmine with leafy splendours of Magnolia, lay in lavish waste upon the gravel, and the air was full of the curious pungency of ivy leaves. Pruning days are my delight, when the laurel and box are trimmed, and the aroma of them scents the whole place, and clipped sprigs fall, and are spread about, strewing the ground as if for some garden triumph. One day last spring (it was on May 12) I thought to try a little pruning on my own account, and severed a long healthy branch of vine, which, when in leaf, would smother a young pomegranate growing on the south wall. I shall never forget what followed the rash act. The vine began to bleed ; pure crystal sap welled up, and drop after drop fell fast ; it flowed and flowed and poured from the wound, and never ceased till seven days and nights were past. In the first dismay at seeing this wine of life pour forth I tried to staunch it by binding a handkerchief tightly round. But that availed nothing ; the cambric was drenched in a moment, while down the stem the stream ran on as the poor Vine wasted her blood upon the earth. I felt it was murder, and the vine seemed to me like some hapless human creature bleeding to death ! Through the day I returned again and again, and guiltily crept to the place at night when the moon was shining— and still the wound bled, and the stem of the vine grew black with moisture, and the wood strawberry leaves underneath were full of big drops. At last one happy morning the tree was dry. I believe it is only in spring that a vine will behave like this—and no harm was done ! But for me henceforth, the vine may go unpruned for evermore. The amateur knife does,

however, still work usefully on young
limes and such-like, keeping the stems
smooth and free from buddings out of
leaves and twigs, and the Gardener is
lenient with my amusements in this line.

In the Wilderness (so we name a rather
wild unkept grassy place outside the gates
of old Italian ironwork that enclose a
broad opening between yew hedges) we
have planted climbing roses, and Clematis
Jackmanni and Montana at the foot of
some useless apple and plum trees. Many
old roses are at their best only when thus
grown wild, as it were, without the least
restraint. Only in this way do they attain
their fulness of grace and beauty. And by
this kind of growth only can one imagine
the sleeping Titania, quite over-canopied
with musk roses. A white Noisette left
to itself to grow up the stem of our stone
pine has grown so immensely in the few
years since it was planted as to take complete possession of the tree ; climbing in
the richest luxuriance up to the top, and
thence hanging down in long rosy wreaths
of exquisite lightness. Yet, although in

its season of flowering none would deny this rose's loveliness, we have hardened our hearts, and have been cutting away the half of it, so as entirely to free the foliage of the pine. There is many a handsomer tree we could easier spare from the garden than the remains of that old Stone Pine. The interests belonging to it are endless. There are the great green cones that reign secure in the widespread umbrella top, and the brown ones that come down with a thump on the grass when the wind blows a gale, and that are good to fill the empty grates in summer, and to smell of Italy in winter; and the titmice and wrens and robins and all manner of small birds that lodge in its branches, whose ways are so pleasant and past finding out; and the curiosity that is never satisfied as to the enormous white fleshy grubs we sometimes see them dig out of holes and crannies in the bark, and carry off in their beaks. And the long double pine needles which drop and lie flat all day where they fell, and bristle upright in the turf next morning after the worms have been pulling them under all night. All these and countless small matters besides make up a little world of interest in our great Pine. The seeds are collected yearly, and they always grow when sown, and thrive up to a certain age ; yet we have not been able to rear any young trees.

In the Boccage there are now two living proofs of the mild weather we have had. The unconscious obstinacy of one of them sometimes makes me smile : it is a Tritoma. December came too soon, and caught the central flower-stalk with its usual pyramid of buds still incomplete. The plant remained in the same position quite unconcerned, and has managed ever since to keep life in the buds, holding itself doggedly upright, and in perfect health, with a sheaf of fresh green leaves about it, and actually surrounding itself with a family of shorter flower-stalks ; and after sometimes looking pale in snow-time or frost, the whole group takes heart again vigorously. With a little sunshine we should see it in nearly as fine bloom as in September. Near the grass walk, glowing in bright pink against the grey of a shadowy elm-tree background, there has been for three weeks or more a large round half-opened Rose : it blooms at the end of a long summer rose-shoot. In the wintry winds it has swung to and fro undismayed. Once or twice I have seen it crested with frost. The white crystals fell away and left it bright as ever when warmer days brought to it a new warmth of colour. Now it begins to flag; the pink petals have gradually hardened, and some of the green leaves are withered; but yet the half-opened rose endures bravely, and sometimes shines like a rosy star. The violet leaves, in sheltered places under the walls, are just beginning to be strewn with amethysts; and the double lilac Marie Louise violets, which we turned out in the borders, have borne flowers as large and fragrant as those in the frames all through the winter. If the old gardening books may be believed, it is quite easy to double the single purple wild Violet.

MARCH

III

MARCH

'March comes in with an Adder's head,
And goes out with a Peacock's tail.'
Old Saying.

MARCH 12.—I waste my time just now in observing from the window, a pair of little blue titmice. They mean to build in the ivy and roses that cluster round the old stone pine ; not, I think, in the rustic bark mansion placed ready for them in a yew tree hard by. These titmice are the gracefulest little things imaginable : flitting about like airy living leaves, their colour a lovely grey-green flashed with blue. One never tires of following with the eye their pretty graceful movements, while they are hunting in and out of the branches. Nothing can exceed their animation and grace as they turn and twist upon a small square of bacon-fat* made fast to the end of a long string. This dainty, replaced constantly as it wastes, hangs all the winter from the tree for the tomtits' special benefit. They are tame also, and, like all very little birds, are seemingly not able to take in the idea of a large human being. Quite unlike this small fearlessness of titmice is the impudent effrontery of our little ne'er-do-weels—the sparrows. Their familiarity seems to have no touch of kindliness in it. I do not blame them. It is the shape of their blunt coarse beaks, that affects their whole nature! The sparrows' perverseness increases, and the friendlier we are to them, the worse they behave. They tear up into shreds our beautiful purple and yellow crocuses, but mainly the yellow. The white and the lilac are left comparatively unmolested, and they seem to attack the beds only in full sunshine. Crocuses, I feel sure, never before suffered from sparrows as they do this season.

* At the time this was written, in 1884, we had not invented cocoa-nuts—a pleasanter feast, and equally acceptable to the tits.

The Sea Purslane also, which luxuriates
in our warm soil, has been persecuted all
the winter, and is now stripped nearly bare
of leaves. I believe this ferocity (for it is
nothing less) of our sparrows is to be
attributed to the unusual dryness of the
weather following the long drought of
last summer. Want of food it cannot be,
for all our beloved birds have been fed
throughout the winter. Moisture is sought
by them in the honey-drop within the
crocus flower, and in the rather fleshy
foliage of the sea purslane. In the spring
the sparrows will amply pay for the sorrows
they cause us now, and the more sparrows'
nests, the fewer grubs there will be to plague
us. It is remarkable that the Gardener is
not unfriendly to our sparrows. In his
judgment their extreme cleverness hides a
multitude of sins. They have now actually
set to work to master the Indian corn
which we give to the pigeons in the hope
that sparrows will never find the way to
swallow it. Their perseverance in trying to
get at the core of it, without holding down
the grain as anyone else would, with one

foot, is worthy of a better cause. The sparrow's eye for colour (one would guess that flaunting yellow would be their chosen colour!) is not the same as the hive-bee's. Bees seem to avoid the yellow Crocus, while they love the white, the purple, and the striped. I have watched them of late when the sun has been warm and bright. I do not know if hive-bees carry on into the summer their objection to yellow; it is certain, however, that in sunflower time the yellow sunflowers are visited by Humble-bees only. One division of our crocus enemies has been partly check-mated by the simple plan of putting in the bulbs very deep; the mice do not quite so easily get at them.* Numbers have also been successfully trapped. Hares, on the other hand, have annoyed us more than usual. A long row of fine young wall-flowers have been devoured by them, besides scores of carnations in the Boccage —the hares and I agreeing in our love for wallflowers, only *their* fancy is for the

* A more successful plan is to stretch black thread from little sticks across the flowers.

leaves, not the flowers. Poor hares! It is little consolation for our loss to remember that they were all shot and roasted for dinner, after they had done the mischief!

Charming as masses and lines of crocus are in the borders and parterres, to enjoy them thoroughly they must be growing in the green grass, and they must be spreading themselves wide open to the sunshine at mid-day. The orchard is gay with broad patches of yellow crocus—remnants torn from the field of the Cloth of Gold ; and the banks of our tiny watercourse is a long green cloth laid out with services of amethyst and silver cups. Within the garden pure white and golden crocus sprinkle the turf round trees and elsewhere, where their leaves need not be mown off too soon.

All this should be in the past tense, for the crocus has already seen its prime, and the remaining few look pinched under the east wind's bane. How strangely vivid, with how great tenacity, will some very little unimportant scene or feeling sometimes cling to the memory through all the years! Thus, with February's first purple crocus, for me unfailingly arises in a far-off tender light the vision of some forgotten garden wilderness enclosed with trees, beyond the town, where my mother and I once walked together. There, as we rested under the trees, appeared before us a solitary purple Crocus, shining on the grassy lawn! After years, whose number one scarcely cares to count, that moment's joy is in sober truth recalled as the most exquisite of a whole long lifetime.

On the old brick south wall of the kitchen garden our only plant of Pyrus japonica is arrayed in finer bloom than usual. Hardly an inch of brown wood shows between the clustering red of a thousand rich and brilliant blossoms. Last autumn the fruit ripened (or, to be truer, hardened) upon it in large green apples of a pippin shape. What an old-fashioned shrub it is! and how seldom seen but in old gardens : and how, in these days, one never thinks of planting a new one. About the roots of the Pyrus japonica, and along the narrow border at the foot of the wall, is a delicious tangle of iris, violets, and rosemary, narcissus of the less common kinds, with many a sweet South-loving plant that has got there one knows not when nor how. Amongst them is a star of Bethlehem, and in the wall itself grow bunches of yellow fumitory (Corydalis lutea) just coming into flower; and there is a seedling holly, and a little starved yew niched in a cranny near the top, and there are patterns in grey lichen scrawled upon the red brick. The polyanthus narcissus, under the wall—roots that have been turned out of the greenhouse after flowering in days gone by—are luxuriantly beautiful this season. Their petals are the clearest yellow, and the cups deep orange, most richly scented. The orange centres seem to gather in and hoard all the sunshine that has ever shone upon them, giving it out again in living sun-gold, even in dullest weather.

The delicate lilac flowers of Iris ensata, sheltered among the thick-growing bushes of dark green leaves, are blooming abundantly. There have been hundreds of

D

blossoms, and we have never been without
them since December, for we had them
under glass all January till February, when
we began to perceive a lilac glow among
the leaves in the open air. These Irises
bloom here at precisely the same time
with those of the same kind in their own
warm sun-steeped land. They could not
flower here so early but for the sheafs of
sheltering leaves which almost hide them
from sight. Few things look more charming for the table than the transiently perfumed iris ensata ! One evening we had
them arranged in knots, with mignonette
and sprays of lemon-scented pelargonium,
toned with the brown of Cryptomeria
elegans. One often hears a gardener's
arrangement of flowers reviled as stiff, or
garish ; yet this lovely contrast of lilac,
green, and brown was only a gardener's
nosegay ! As a decoration it might have
been deemed pallid, but for the presence of
glasses filled with deep coloured primroses, Dog-tooth violets, and Glory of the
snow, all resting against the brown. The
tips of Cryptomeria used in this way are

neither stiff nor heavy, but full of the lightest grace.

MARCH 21.—Spring began this morning * before 6 A.M. The tame robin sang such a brilliant brief fantasia in the magnolia just outside my window, that when the shutters were opened it was a surprise to see heavy snow falling. Snow is as good as change of scene to us home-keeping folk. Our view from the windows is transformed. The large Ilex oak drooping under its load of snow looks more like a yew, or some kind of fir tree. The outline and character of the Stone pine is entirely changed. 'Deborah' and the sun dial stand out boldly sculptured in black and white, as every day they certainly are not. The parterre with its crocuses is gone; the grass and the walks are nowhere. Branching elms in the background are almost as much increased in size by the snow crystalising over every slender twig, as in summer by their leafy millions. But all this proved only a dissolving view : by noon the grass appeared again, green as

* Spring is said to commence 21st March.

an emerald, and the thrushes were loudly rejoicing. The yews will *smoke* no more after such heavy snow! On bright afternoons, chiefly during the earlier part of the month, it was exactly as if smouldering fires burnt within some of them so hidden were they in clouds of smoke. There must have been always a light breeze stirring at the time; yet the air would mostly seem unusually still when this smoke arose. And then, when it cleared off, the yews were like 'dusty millers,' powdered over with pollen. One or two of the younger yews (they never flower profusely until they are many years older) give 'the idea' of bursting into fresh green buds of spring all over them, at the points of almost every twig. Buds, however, they are not, only mischievous imitations; or a sort of gall made by insects (mites). Nothing can be discovered by pulling these buds to pieces; at least, after minute examinations, we have never been able to find the insect inside. When the days are warm and dry I have often worked for an hour or so at one time, pulling off the growths as high as I could reach all round the trees, but the result is small ; they soon come again as thick as ever.

My favourite Garrya elliptica is in beauty now, growing against the east wall of the entrance court. A soft veil of catkins enshrouds the tree from its top downwards ; each long catkin, just tinged with a rosy bloom, is delicately outlined against the dark round-leaved foliage. I can fancy the Garrya standing alone, thus softly veiled, upon the open sward—how beautiful it would be ! But if this ever happens I do not know, for in our climate it seems to need the support or shelter of a wall. I have been going round the garden in the bleak windy sunshine ; and I think our flowers of March are nearly many enough and varied enough to satisfy even *our* immoderate desires.

The straight walk in the kitchen garden never looks fairer, with all its roses, than now in the simple green and gold of daffodil clumps all the way on both sides. All sorts of daffodils are everywhere, from the large heavy headed double ones, to

the diminutive brilliant little Hoop petti-
coat, only three inches high. There is
Pulmonaria, Triteleia, and white violets
and patches of white Arabis, and primroses
just becoming plentiful. There is a long,
blue-rimmed border of Grape Hyacinth, and
another of metallic-shining Scillas. Blue
prevails indeed—blue Scilla and Chiono-
doxa, blue hepatica, blue Omphalodes.
Soon there will be deep blue gentian, beside which all other blues will pale. Dear
little cheerful-eyed Omphalodes! The
old plants have worn themselves out, but
young roots are spreading over some stones
near the Roman Walk, and flowering with
enthusiastic vigour. A charming Hungarian
lady the other day embraced it (so to
speak) with delight. She said Omphalodes verna grew wild in her native woods.
Amongst the rarer gems must be counted
Sisyrinchium grandiflorum, or better
named, Satin-flower, with its exquisitely
shaped purple bells, like hanging crocus
flowers ; and on the rounded south side
of Glorietta is a group of magnificently
fiery, scarlet anemones.

APRIL

IV

APRIL

' " Ay, there's easting in it,"
  The white-haired sailor said,
  As he looked on the sweep of tossing grey
  And the flying flakes of snowy spray,
  Wind-borne o'er the great pier-head.

' " Ay, there's easting in it,"
  Said the herd, who his moor-watch kept ;
  " The lambs crouch clustering under the Oak,
  And last night a sound like sea-waves broke
  As the wind my turf-walls swept." '

APRIL 3.—Yes, 'there's easting in it,' this
dry hard day, under the hard pitiless blue.
Day after day, a cold sun shines down
upon the parched and dusty world. The
sun shines, but there is none of the sove-
reign delight of sunshine. The sky is as
steel and brass; the grass is white with
frost morning after morning, and there has
not fallen one April shower to set the sap

running within the black bare trees and loose the young leaves and blossoms bound up within their hard buds. There is no life in the fields, no balm in the air, 'nothing grows,' as the saying is. Everything looks pinched and unhappy, and I think no living thing enjoys the east wind, except perhaps the skylarks. They, dear souls, spring up and glory in the open heaven above them. They rise quivering and carolling up to the very gates! Doubtless *they* in their joy are singing, 'Blow, thou wind of God!' How beautiful are the daffodils just now; and how their pure cold yellow seems in harmony with the freezing sunshine! But they are none the better for it, and never were there so many imperfect, unaccomplished flowers among them. One or two in every clump come out uncomfortably green, or open unkindly, and as if they could not make up their minds to be either good green leaves, or fair yellow flowers! These unhappy ones are rather amusing, but they are certainly very ugly : 'there's easting in it.' The great mass of daffodils, however,

were never finer. I am comparing the
common single long-tubed daffodil (Tela-
monius plenus) with Sir Watkin. The
former would surely be thought almost the
handsomer of the two, but for Sir Watkin's
star-like corolla and erect carriage. Our
Cernuus, a new possession, is in bloom :
it seems almost too delicate for the open
border. But in the Boccage, there grows
the joy of my eyes, a lovely group of
cream-white daffodils !

The joy of daffodils is not to be forbid,
and their season is the most beautiful
of all the year ! Thus did my heart
decide this very evening as I wandered
amidst a flood of daffodils overflowing
every corner of the garden, surging over
every border, sprinkling every breadth
of green grass, in all the crystal clear-
ness of their yellow gold. The young
moon showered silver all about them, the
thrushes sang aloud their praises far
and near. Millions of daffodils joyously
blooming everywhere. Yet it is certain
that as soon as the gentians come, or the
apple-blossoms, or the hawthorn, or the

rose, I shall feel just the same, and shall say again, ' *This* is the most beautiful time of all !' So was it when crocuses, yellow, white, and purple, burst into splendour in those wintry days of March ; so was it when long lines of Scylla, made the whole garden bluely beautiful. But the intense purity of these daffodils takes the fancy and holds it with a spell more powerful than the magic of all other colours. During sixteen years have the daffodils silently multiplied as they grew in the garden. In all these years the different strains have never mixed. The fine old double-flowering Telamon, still crowds broad reaches of the lawn, with intermingling groups of single long-cupped flowers; the double are still richly double, the single yet remain austerely single— unchanged, and as I believe firmly unchangeable. My favourite star-shaped short-cupped daffodils, however, go on doubling for ever. In sheltered corners there are choice collections of the rarer kinds. There is the coy Princess: Obvalaria and Leedsii, and pallid down-

cast cernuous, etc., etc. Little pumilis is
going off, after taking part in the soft
colour-chord touched by Glory of the
snow (Chionodoxia) blue Hepatica and
Sysirinchium.

On the grass in the orchard, are
wild Lent lilies, transplanted hither
from the sweet wild meadows of Derbyshire. They are modest little things,
most palely delicate in colour, their bent
heads all turned one way, south-east.
There is something peculiarly neat and
pretty in the half-opened bud, the long
tube being *fulled* round the edge as if drawn
in by a thread—a bit of Dame Nature's
neatest needlework! We are trying these
wild ones also in a garden border, but
I do not expect them ever to double.*
In the broad new border of the Boccage
and in the Fantaisie, heavily scented
jonquils flourish in perfect peace, their
deep content plainly visible, as it always is
with some flowers. 'Blue Roses' would

* In 1895, several years after this was written, the
Lent lilies from Derbyshire, planted in the border,
still remain single.—E. V. B.

give one little pleasure ; but how exquisite is the idea of a White Jonquil·! There are times when I am possessed with the wish for coloured flowers to be white. A white Camellia japonica ! a white Chinese currant ! At this moment, however, a crowd of pure white daffodils is the desire of my heart. In the garden of our castle in Spain there shall be a long green walk, bordered thickly on each side, under the pomegranate trees, with white and golden daffodils, both single and double.

In the orchard there is a green walk where one passes through the shimmering pink of large bushes of Chinese or Californian currant (ribes sanguineum). As yet they are only in rosy bud ; but there is something fairy-like in the extreme lightness of these interlacing branches, tipped with clustered points of pink ; it is better than when the flowers are full, for·then a little green begins also to show and there is something gone from the beauty of them. Better still than the magic of this roseate mist, there is a certain sweet and silvery charm begun to spread over all the garden, quite low on the ground, almost under foot. The seeds may have lain there long, first carried by the birds, perhaps. We have never before observed this overspreading of White Violets. In every corner where there may be any little bit of border not dug—under trees, even niched into the walls—in all parts of the garden are white violets. We should not be content with always white instead of purple; yet there is some kind of strange little spell about the white, so that sometimes I am compelled to put on my hat and hasten out into the garden, just for a moment's look at their fresh pleasant faces, and to inhale their scent. There is no 'easting' in their perfume, whether they come white or blue! and indeed I think these white violets must be here 'for luck!' It matters not if we have to-day's chill sunlight, or if a black north-easter blows, the silvery violet patches shine on unheeding in serene and genial lowliness. Ah, how ungrudgingly would we not—if this might be—pass them on into the grey life of one or two, to cheer them for a space, when they sigh, 'Ay, there's easting in it,' . . . . sighing sadly

'O for the perfect work of time ;
O for the other shore !
Where the riddles of years are read at last
And the east wind blows no more.'

Violets are very little flowers, but somehow there's much to say about them ! Under a sunny hedgerow of the Walk meadow, blue and white violets grow together, with a third kind in which the blue seems to run into the white ; white violets dashed with blue or lilac. And two or three years ago under another quickset hedge in our lane, I scattered some seeds of purple violets for the delight of our village children, or for any little wayfarers in the spring. The seeds did not seem to come up, and I forgot all about them till the other day, when we saw, with great satisfaction, a little boy and his big brother happily engaged gathering dark sweet Violets under the barren hedge, and making them up into posies with a few scant early daisies. I sowed many seeds

that year along our dull roadside banks—
common things that might well have
grown, and I counted on the children's
pleasure and surprise when they found
such lovely things in bloom—there were
Campanulas and Stocks and Poppies,
Snapdragons, Primroses, Foxgloves, and
yellow Broom, and Virginian Stock. But
never a plant came up, excepting just one
foxglove, whose fine spire of buds was
untimely plucked—and now the violets.

I do not know if the east wind has to
answer for our Forget-me-nots coming
red. Most of the blue is more freely mixed
with pink than usual, and one root, under
a chestnut tree near the water-course, has
fairly gone into deep crimson. If the seeds
can be saved, we might possibly get from
them a new variety. But a crimson forget-me-not would be unpoetical, and un-
real, and like the dark blue which appeared
a few years ago, interesting only as a
curiosity. There was some failure in the
seed last year, so that our *pavé of turquoise*
will not this season be quite so extensive
as usual. Brilliant and close-flowering,

E

however, as our garden Myosotis* is, the pleasure of it never could compare with the image—glassed I suppose in almost every heart—of the clear quiet pool, set in some sequestered meadow, on whose green margin grew the blue forget-me-not. Or of the place where it bloomed just out of reach in the little stream among wavering weeds, shedding starlets of heaven's blue upon the water under the willows. Those were the real *Vergessmeinnicht* of our youth, and when we sat on the bank beside them, or wet our feet in gaining difficult possession of them, we thought then upon the dear old half-sad, half-foolish German romance — never remembered in the garden plots.

APRIL 13.—At last a gracious rain has fallen. A sort of quickening thrilled at once through all the garden, and now the grass gives out a green answer to the precious drops. There is to-day at the southern end of the broad walk—in the untidy—because too full—border facing the east, a new beautiful colour of Pæonies in

* Myosotis dissitiflora

their first young growth. I do not remember them before the rain; now the
strong healthy stalks pushing up above the
ground are a full crimson red. The colour
is so vivid, it almost has the effect of some
strange flowers, seen from a little distance.
At the opposite end of the walk the onion
flavour of the Crown Imperials is not so
unpleasantly perceptible as it sometimes
has been. I remember it was long before
we discovered the source of the strong
odour pervading that part of the garden.
Not an onion anywhere near ; there seemed
nothing to account for it. Gerard says,
'the whole plant do savour or smell very
like a fox.' I think we may well forgive
our crown imperials their smell, however,
for the stately show they make ; and if
taste and fashion did not change with
flowers as with other things, they might
still be among the choice favourites of
spring. Ours ought to be somewhat taller,
a fine Crown Imperial should rise so high
that a little child might stand under the
yellow bells and look up into the moon-
stone circlet within ; for 'in the bottom of

each of these bells there is placed six drops of most clear shining sweet water, in taste like sugar.'   In another place are also saffron-coloured crown imperials, coming into bloom.   They are commoner and less beautiful than the yellow.

This is the legend of the crown-imperial, or Pearl Lily. ' Jesus walked in the garden of Gethsemane.—And the lily we call the crown-imperial lily, had just been crowned.   And when all the other flowers bowed their heads as the Saviour passed along, she alone refused to bend, and held up her head quite straight and stiff.   Jesus laid His hand upon the flower and gently said, "Lily, lily, be not so proud ! "   Ever since the flowers of the crown-imperial have bent down all round and have stood so, filled with tears.'

I never dwell upon failures in the garden : they are never many, and are soon forgotten.   Here may be the place, however, to record one small disappointment.   Round the stone floor of the garden porch, we had made an outer rim of gold and silver Thyme.   The intention

was, that with every passing step, crossing
over to the gravel, or with the sweep of
a trailing gown, should arise sweet thymy
odours on the air. But the thing did not
succeed. The gold and silver thyme all
died away before any one had enjoyed it
much. And yet perhaps, the idea is
worthy of another trial. Perhaps thyme
or wild mint might be induced to grow
upon the lawn, and in the mowing or the
treading it would smell deliciously. A
trimly shaped Rosemary in bloom, is about
as pleasant a sight as can well be seen on
an April day. The 'sweet gaping flowers'
of a bluish-grey, set not too thickly among
the dark green narrow leaves, give such
a sense of neatness ; they look so clean
and cool, that the wonder is the sweet-
smelling shrub should not be a greater
favourite. Two hundred years ago it seems
to have been planted in every garden.
Then there were gilded rosemarys, and
Rosemary of the poets, and several wild
rosemarys—all grown for physical or civil
purposes. It was used at weddings, and
funerals, and a bundle of it was a welcome

gift bestowed upon friends. Where rosemary flourishes nigh the house, there the
wife is said to rule. It is by no means for
any such reason, however, that so shapely
and fine a bush of it grows beside our
south porch! It is because it worships the
sun, and when the sun shines the bees are
about it all day long.

> *'The life that throbs in April's heart*
> *Wakes every mortal thing ;*
> *And grief, with birds and buds and flowers*
> *Stirs freshly in the Spring.'*
>
> *Burns.*

M A Y

V

MAY-DAY EVE IN THE MORNING

' Well may I guess and feel
Why Autumn should be sad,
But vernal airs no sorrow feel,
Spring should be gay and glad.'—*Keble.*

THE hour from 8 to 9 A.M. is often the quietest in all the day. Everybody has gone to breakfast, and the garden is deserted. Thrushes and blackbirds are breakfasting all over the meadow, and the distant singing heard among the further elm trees gives emphasis to the nearer silence. Even the bees are gone home to breakfast; only here and there a lumbering old humble-bee grumbles alone in the blossoming fruit trees. It is time for the young nestlings' second or third meal, and the tame robin redbreast (who, though it is no longer winter, still visits the window) is hurriedly packing a slender worm in her bill, and then, by the direction of her flight

betrays the cherished secret of her treasure.
Yet it must be confessed that when the air
is less chilly the hour is often fuller of mur-
muring stir among the birds and bees than
it is to-day.

> ' The small bees busy at their threshold old,
>   And lambs lamenting in their four-fold fold.

Cold as it is, there is one tall white Iris—just
one among a thousand budding now in
double file throughout the garden—carefully, slowly opening.   It rises above all the
other irises—first and fairest, as the first of
every flower is—and to-morrow it will be
full-blown, in honour of the day.   The eve
of May-Day should be full of mysteries in
earth and air.   A great change is approach-
ing, and all Nature knows it.   I myself but
dimly guess and feel what it may be.   It may
be that the birth of summer is at hand, and
already a few of Nature's loveliest children
' haste to die.'   Snowdrops are forgotten,
and primrose-tide is fading from the woods.
Under the yellow Berberis yellow petals
lie in little heaps or lines of yellow drift :
and every pearly bud on the white cherry
trees has opened wide.   There is no wind,

but they will not last; another day or two
and the fruit will be set, and we shall see
twin cherries swelling greenly all over each
long length of blossomed bough.

Either to-day, or on May-day, one ought
to see the fairies, according to the old
Scottish legends! No fairies appeared
this time, but I saw a good deal between
eight and nine, looking from the broad
walk, upon our old kitchen garden walls,
bright with the eastern sun. How shall
the charm of these old brick walls be
described? Words could never paint it.
In the clear glow of morning light, the reds
are so delicately pure and warm, and they
are mottled with such varied greys and
many-tinted yellows. There are stout old
buttresses, too, mossed and ferny, and grey
with eld. Ancient rugged pear trees grow
up against it; and their outstretched
knotted old limbs are set now with knots of
flowers, and young, tender leaves, and the
half-transparent shadow of every flower
and leaf lies still, or trembles on the wall.
One of these pear trees, quite worn out
and decayed with age, had been cleared

away last winter, leaving a broad vacant space, a space that is not bare, but full of interest. Little incidents and details, unobserved before, were plainly seen this morning. There is a curious arrangement of wood - bricks built in regular order amongst the others. Worm-eaten and decayed, they have weathered to the same colour as the greyer of the bricks, and are so inconspicuous as to pass usually unremarked. These wood-bricks must have been devised for the more careful nailing up of fruit trees. The fine new garden walls of those days might not be disfigured with nails! some have fallen out, leaving recesses convenient for wrens' and other nests. Suddenly appeared a curved line of bricks, set end-wise, showing where once had been a low-browed narrow door-way, bricked up long since. There is another as low and narrow, faintly visible farther down. Carlyle wrote of the days 'when dresses were smaller and thoughts were larger.' Certainly our modern door-ways are mostly wider than those of older date.

The old walls, with the sunlight dis-

covering upon them traces of Time's land-
marks, are enough to set one dreaming
of those former days, and for the moment
it is easy to live in many a bygone scene ;
to fancy the precise training of the fruit
trees to the wood-blocks; the daily traffic
through that little doorway. One could
see the gardeners with their quaint old-
fashioned wheel - barrows and watering-
pots going in and out; and I recalled the
day named in Evelyn's Diary, when
George Evelyn and his cousin John
Evelyn of Sayes Court, walked through
the door together—George, showing his
gardens with due pride—John, with grave
observant eye, noting how they were
'exquisitely kept though large.' That
afternoon was July 23, 1679. The sunny
wall stood then in deep shade on this
side, and where now, on May Eve, two
centuries after, Pear blossoms whiten all
over it, George Evelyn's young trees were
ripening their first fruits. Along the top
of the wall grow wild grasses and crested
moss. There is a plant of Shepherd's
Purse with glorious spread of seed and

flower, luxuriating up there in lofty, safe seclusion. Seen from below, so freshly green against the blue, these wild things do—to us—enhance the picturesqueness of the old wall ; and while looking up at them thus, one feels in some degree that curious sense of infinity, the reason of which no one ever has explained. The Evelyns in their day would have treated them as unruly weeds, and would have made short work with them. Not half-an-hour hence, when the Traveller turns the corner, and his gold face looks the other way, the old door and the wooden bricks with the vision of that summer day two hundred and five years back, will fade fast and be lost in shadow. Another old wall on the other side of the lawn is also propped at intervals with heavy buttresses. The aspect is north, and on these rude masses of old brick grow my wild gardens. The buttresses are gnarled and irregularly scored and furrowed by huge ivy stems veiled under moss and lichen.

The finest of the two ' gardens ' is that one nearest Syringa and the greenhouse door. There, a Nut tree of 6 inches, and a Yew 3 inches high, are thrown into the shade by two great Moon Daisies and a giant Broom. These are my forest trees! The broom don't care for so much cold shade, and every season makes rampant efforts to reach above it and catch the sun upon its golden plumes. It is all but at the top now. If I look down very closely a miniature landscape may be discerned— strips of flower garden inwoven with a wild scene of mossy caves and deep ravines. The edges of all these tiny fissures are at this time faintly blue with eyebright of microscopic littleness. One must almost use a glass to see plainly the tiny perfect flowers, no bigger than a pin's head, with little leaves and stalks to match. Delicate small grasses overhang the mouth of the caverns, where small wild beasts of insect race lie lost after their night of rapine. Weird jungles of grey Cup-moss and lichen skirt the garden side, and sheaves of mimic bulrush wave gold-brown heads in a morass of greenest moss; and then we come upon a brilliant little daisy, every stalk a-flower

in the very perfection of blithe good
humour, though not one single ray of sunshine has ever touched its silver.   A rather
coarse Polipody fern in part supports the
daisy's roots, and one or two more tender
ferns droop gently near it.   The group is
fringed below with a lilac patch of chance-
sown aubrietia.   Perhaps a scarlet wood
strawberry will ripen late on the tufted
pink runners that are always climbing
higher up the buttress; and I shall soon
look for the pretty Draba verna, which
with one or two sister weeds—all micro-
scopically small—will in their courses
bloom and fade here through the summer;
that is, if they are not overtaken by the
drought already threatening.

Along the upper ledges young leaves of
Cymbalaria are coming thick and fast.
This lovely well-known little antirrhinum
is more or less common all over Europe,
I believe, however named — whether
Mother of Thousands, as in the old stone
fences of Somersetshire, or in Scotland
Wandering Sailor, or the Fronde della
Madonna of the rocks and carved pedi-

ments of Italy. Wherever old stone or marble is, there—with the universal pellitory—we find the sweet enrichment of our toad-flax.* Soon it will be breaking in avalanches all down the old buttress, and at close of summer a thick green curtain will have long been drawn over my small enchanted wild.

MAY 21.—To-day there is heavy rain, and the Gardener has just come in to announce the first blooming of a new Iris. A plant of pale grey iris was given to me last summer, and we have looked anxiously for its flowering. The Iris procession begins this year with the white and purple in lavish profusion. They flower together for the first time, alternately, along the line of holly hedge. The purple are too impatient usually to wait for the blooming of the white. These stand now in multitudes under the dining-room windows, and along the south-walk. Someone has compared them to the company of St

---

* Among the stones of 'the Roman walk' occurs another and more lovely variety. A. Pilosa, is its distinguishing name.

F

Ursula's white-robed virgins.   Our irises begin to know that they are especial favourites here, and their great size, and luxuriance is bewildering. Of course ' *they* ' would tell me it is only because their roots have 'become established,' as they say. Both Ensata and the Fleur-de-Lys bear forcing well, and we have never been without either since January. The fine broad foliage of the fleur-de-lys was welcome, for its masses of fresh green in winter, when the flowering plants were brought into the house. The white flowers send forth, however, when thus forced, a fragrance that some find too powerful; as Gerard says of lilac, 'troubling and molesting the head in a strange manner, with a ponticke and unacquainted savour.'

It is strange that Iris germanica, whose scent I have sometimes known at Rome (and notably where it grows round the tomb of Cæcilia Metella) to make the sweet air still more delicious, has here no kind of scent. A pleasant change of colour comes, near the entrance court : it is purple iris growing with a clump of amber-edged yellow tulips. And still more refined and lovely is the contrast upon a south wall, of a large flowered mauve clematis, with Gloire de Dijon rose and the brown shoots of flexuosa honeysuckle intermixed with white iris below. The tulips in the tulip parterre are over, after a brilliant existence of nearly four weeks. One day they were seen to shine like lamps of coloured fire, through the thinner spaces of a large black Irish yew. The beautiful effect never returned again ; it was perhaps due to some strange accident of light. Light does often use 'lawful magic' marvellously under the pure intensity of a morning sky, or just before the sun goes down. I have seen the Phillyreas in the garden in the early hours, reflect back positive blue from their dark foliage, and there is a Persian lilac in bloom whose colour is gorgeous at such a time. It is absolutely dazzling. Birds, too, flash past with colours that might vie with those of oriental plumage. Green-finches on the wing or among the branches are emerald-green like real green parrots, or a titmouse flits from tree to tree in 'azurn sheen,' as blue as any kingfisher. It is the way the sun strikes at this sweet hour. At sunset I have seen the great elms all glorious within, the straightness of their massive stems burning with a lurid glow from root to treetop behind the leaves ; and last evening when, after the rain, the sunset shone upon a cypress, a million rain-drops twinkling all over it became lustrous diamonds of the purest water, darting long rays of rainbow hues.

No springtime could ever be more perfect in its outward beautifulness than this May is, though indeed the rain and cold do somewhat spoil our full enjoyment. It must have been in a spring like this that Jean Paul wrote of 'winter painted green.' Yet there were days when the perfume of apple blossoms was borne through all the garden as balmily as if the breezes had not been ice. Never were apple trees more snowily, rosily radiant. It was as beautiful as a dream to pass along underneath their flower laden branches ; and so abundant was the bloom that when it fell the petals lay so thick upon the grass that the thrushes tripped up and stumbled in their haste to run through it! Lilac, too—a more lasting pleasure—is in finer bloom than ever I remember it. Lilacs do not usually take the place they are worthy of in our gardens. In former days, when the 'Blew-pipe tree' was a novelty, they planted it in the front ranks ; but now, somehow, it seems always pushed out of the way, and yet the loveliness of lilac trees in May can be scarcely equalled, while one feels that the first whiff of their perfume in the garden is as the very heart and soul of memory. Our old trees at the back of the Broad Walk border are scarcely seen from the garden. They cheerfully give their beauty to the other side, overhanging the tarred paling of the potting-house yard, and glorifying its business-like surroundings with a world of fragrant colour. From an upper window of the house I look down upon a distant view of this tossing sea of lilac.

Two or three young lilac bushes were planted a few years back in the orchard ;

they are better placed : one can enjoy them more intimately, walk round them, or pull down a branch to smell the lilac cones. But our white lilac, most refined and loveliest of all, grows nowhere unencumbered with shrubbery.

If the forest of the Fantaisie were but half a mile round instead of half a rood, it would be perfect. Its position gives variety, that quality which charms as much in a garden as does the play of expression in a human face. It is as if in following the green garden ways we went ' from grave to gay, from lively to severe.'

From the sunny masses of pink and white Phlox repens, blue Gentian, and narcissus poeticus, in the wildest profusion, ending in a wholly indescribable glow of azalea mollis, the path winds along smooth grass, and close-trimmed laurel into the woodland shade, between great clumps of purple iris growing among stones and flints, over-run with stonecrop, violas, and fumitory. Here, though so tiny that some one the other day, took it for a child's garden, there is something of the dim quiet

of a wood. Every wild plant that makes
its home in it is welcome ; even dande-
lions, and stellaria, and wood - sorrel
(flower of the Holy Ghost), one little flower
of which has just remembered it is Whit-
suntide, and opened its veined petals.

The bluebells nodding to each other
under this sun-chequered living green of
Spring, are fresh joy to me every morning
and every evening. I suppose wide sheets
of them, a very 'Heaven upbreaking from
the earth,' might give greater pleasure ;
but only in extent—scarcely in degree.
My 'wood' is but a little chink of heaven,
yet the delight of it is as pure as it is
small. There was a fear lest these wild
hyacinths might deteriorate in land not
poor enough to keep them humble ; that
downward curve of the slender stalk, which
is grace itself and the glory of bluebells,
seemed about to be lost in over-luxuri-
ance ; the heads of flower, bent low
enough however, after they were fully
blown. There are countless groups of
white, and blue, and pale mauve hyacinths
that once were wild, dispersed about the

borders ; but the cultivated ground seems to give a certain fatness to leaf, and stalk, and flower, which takes just so much off from their perfect beauty.

Coming out of the wood, a sharp turn to the left leads one into a fair round green, and 'Glorietta' smiles out of the enclosing thicket. Parrot tulips flaunt in yellow and scarlet rags, amid purple iris and red anemones, round one-half of the charmed circle ; the other half, being turned from the sun, can only boast of late green buds. A deeper interest lies in the junipers above the budding tulips, for there the birds build, and know themselves secure.

JUNE

VI

THE JUNE GARDEN

'The whispering of the boding trees
The deep-toned music of the soul.'

'One hour with thee, when burning June
Waves her red flag at pitch of noon;'

JUNE is the most beautiful month in all the year. There is nothing like it. After years of wavering choice between autumn and the spring—which might be best—the decision is made, and the question, in my own mind at least, at rest for ever, on this green June morning. There is nothing else on earth that ever can compare with beautiful, flowery, flowerful June! The colour of the leaves is exquisite, and as perfect is the colour of the shade they cast. After June is past it will be different, since the leaves will no longer then be thinly half-transparent ; but now on this glorious

1st of June, the sun shines down upon the trees from his throne of cloudless blue, and there is no shade ; it is all green sunshine under the trees. The green, when many-tinted summer is new, if not so brilliant as autumnal gold and red, is yet sufficiently various to satisfy the eye. The olive-green of young oak, and poplar, and ash, contrasts with the fresher greens of elm and lime. I remember an old Somerset-shire woman, who used to say, the woods in June were like a piece of 'lady's em-broidery work.' To-day the hedgerow elms and lines of distant wood are lustrous. No other word could give so well this wonderful glow of June upon the leaves, and only a poet could have found the word ! * And then when the sun is down, and the glowing trees are by contrast dim and solemn, and the soft 'tur-turring' of the turtle-doves in the thorn tree in the field is hushed, I know that I shall find the white Irises more shining in their polished whiteness than during all the day, filling

* 'Slides the bird o'er lustrous woodland, etc.'— *Tennyson.*

the air with perfume. In the garden, we
have gold as rich as October ever gave ;
and we have silver which is June's alone.
Laburnums rain gold above the golden
broom, and intermix with Silvern heaps
of white-thorn and silvery broom. And
when did ever autumnal-mellowed beech
light up the yellow groves with velvet fires,
so softly red as the young shoots of copper
beech, which scatter now their spray of
rubies and clear jacinth, dropping down
between us and the sun? And when did
autumn ever burn with such crimsons as
glow in these scarlet double thorns, or in
the piled-up splendours of rhododendron,
which now illuminate the woods ?

The yews and yewen hedges have put
on a new face, and conceal all trace of
gloom beneath young leaves of russet-
gold. Yet there is regret and grief this
beautiful June morning ! I find myself
quoting Wordsworth, saying to myself,
' There is a change, and I am poor ' ; for
the whole garden is all jubilant with song,
but the song that is best is not heard.
There is no nightingale this year. We

listen and watch in vain. Sometimes
some thrush singing notes of unwonted
fire and sweetness will for a moment deceive
the ear : this has happened once or twice.
But when indeed the nightingale sings,
he is never mistaken for a thrush. What
alas ! is the mysterious cause of our loss?
We are fain to hope it may be the cold
winds of May and April; because there are
no glowworms; or because there is so little
oak about the place. (Oak scrub must this
autumn be planted somewhere.) Anything
is better to believe than the ugly reason
of bird-stealers. Whatever the reason be—

> 'Such change, and at the very door
> Of my fond heart, hath made me poor,'

Of a winter garden it is easy enough to
write. But in June ! the garden in midsummer ! Out of the fulness of it how is
choice to be made of one bright flower for
praise more than another ? It is a world of
surpassing beauty. This morning, in the
still shade of a south window, one small
petal dropped upon the window-sill from
a flowery branch of cotoneaster (*Good
Neighbour*). One is seldom present just at

the very moment when a petal falls. The flower may wither or be shaken in the wind, or fall at a touch, and the leaves be scattered. But when both shape and colour are unchanged, and yet the petals drop quietly one by one in some profound calm of a summer dawn or evening twilight, there is pathos in it. The flower is not dead, but her time has come. The flowers of the cistus family, which are now delighting us, quite literally have their day. In the morning there is a mass of bloom; at evening not a single flower remains. The sole trace left is a pink or white or yellow mosaic, where the falling petals have showered down upon the grass or gravel. The difficulty is, to find room enough for cistus. They require some bank or lengths of rock garden, to be given up entirely to them. Then there might be a blaze of colour through all the summer, in favourable weather, for they do not like too much rain. In proportion to the brief individual existence of the Cistus flowers are their innumerable buds. And they are as costless as they are lovely ; a few packets of seed will stock a garden! Once we had the pink Riviera cistus of the large grey-green leaves and exquisite flowers which light up the hills and dusty roadsides like rose-coloured lamps alive in broad daylight! Our plants perished in some unusually severe frost. The white cistus, with narrower, more polished, aromatic foliage, is hardier, and seems quite happy here in a south aspect. We have but one old Gum Cistus, as fragile, and more wondrously beautiful than all the rest. How the folds and crumples in the satin of her ample petal do but enhance her beauty! It grows on the lawn at the foot of a Noisette rose that now envelopes the bare stem of a dead weeping ash. The rose climbed up to the top of the tree, and falls over in a great luxuriance of flower and leaf and thorn. Within the thorniest heart of this thorny rose-thicket a thrush has her nest. I think, in her wisdom, she this time made it just a little *too* safe. The young thrushes still sit full fledged in the nest; I think they dare not tempt the thorns.

As we pass through the south porch the

martin from her mud hut over the door
skims out into the sunshine. When she
begins to sit there will be little time for
these wide sweeps of flight, or to idle upon
the Rose arches, twittering and preening
those long, blue-black wings of hers! On
either side the porch there grows a
lavender bush and a rosemary. The
lavender is failing, as it did last summer.
The bud-stalks look quite firm and healthy
up to a certain point, and then each head
hangs down and in a little while they
look withered and black—as if they were
strangled. 'Some failure at the root,' is
the Gardener's verdict for this and many
another unpleasantness in the garden.
Is it not mostly 'failure at the root' in
many of our mistakes outside the garden?
None of the other lavender plants seem
affected in the same way, fortunately.
Ferns and a fine root of Turncap Lily
grow at the back of the lavender, and up
the porch wall is a young Banksia rose
climbing apace, and flowering for the first
time. It ought to have been yellow, but
it has come white. Under the rosemary

G

is a great old conch shell, kept filled with
fresh water for the birds. The narrow
border that runs along under the Oak-
room window is my trouble and my dear
delight. I hope nothing will ever lead me
to call it a '·herbaceous border!' It has
become so much the fashion to call everything herbaceous which is not 'bedding
out,' that the meaning of the word is
usually lost sight of, and all kinds'of woody
perrenials are, so it seems to me, included
in the 'herbaceous border.' The phrase
also seems to leave out all the poetry of
the garden. Not, I think, more than a
dozen or fifteen years old, it dates from
the first rage for yellow calceolarias and
pyrethrums and the carpetings, when
'herbaceous' things were admitted only
somewhere out of the way by sufferance.
May this be the first and last time I
have to write 'Herbaceous border!'

Under the window a cotoneaster bears
good promise of its pink liliputian apple
crop for the blackbirds in October. And
then there is a little wilderness of wood
strawberries. They want to have it all

their own way here, and mean to get it.
They smother the hepaticas, and choke
the irises, and over-reach the turf verge;
and then ground-Ivy stretches along and
over the strawberries, and has to be
quickly made an end of. Red wood-straw-
berries are ripening for the children, mixed
with a few of the yellow-flowered fragaria
indica, whose berry is very handsome, but
so acrid as to ensure its stay safe enough
on its stalk. Neither child nor bird would
taste a second time. Italians, with their
characteristic gentle fun call it 'Inganna
Donna.' Vine and pomegranate and
white French honeysuckle, clematis and
Eccremocarpus, grow up in more or less of
wild luxuriance around the window. The
pomegranate never yet has flowered,
though her sister plant (since dead) in
another part of the garden used to flame
with blossom. Were it possible to decide
which to like best of all these, one or two
at least might attain perfection. It ought
perhaps to be the pomegranate, and a
clear place should be made for it. But
none of the others can be sacrificed; and

indeed I wish for a pyracantha and a Ceanothus (for its blue), and a hundred others, to be added. Then there come the Star of Bethlehem and Pink Convolvulus and a line of stately white Lilies which always bloom well; and just now brilliant roses upon unpruned trees, in gadding wreaths of beauty, stray above the strawberry leaves, with a sullen glow of yellow and purple iris (Darius) between the wreaths. This tall Iris defied the overmastering luxuriance about their roots, while the beautiful 'Versailles' was discouraged and withdrew herself.

There is aromatic Santolina and woodruff and Japan anemone, all mixed up, and entangled with the wood strawberries, and the border ends at a pink wall—pink with great hanging bunches of the old china rose. Right in front, indifferent alike to strawberries and all the world, are three Euphorbias. Of their own good will and choice they grow up here. It would be cruel to uproot them, they stand so firm and grand in their placid self assertion. I do not love them, but they compel my

regard. It has been remarked of them
that they are beautiful, from the decision of character they display. Even from
seed, they know how they intend to grow,
and they complete their plan. There is
the smooth firm stem, straight as a line, in
colour emerald washed with amethyst, and
the narrow leaves, exactly matched in size,
placed with perfect symmetry up the stem
till they reach the four-branched seed-
holders, which proceed like a branching
capital from the top of the green tall
pillar. The seed-holders on the four
branches support leaves of another shape in
ordered pairs, and each pair guards a
poisonous-looking flower or seed. From
first to last there is not a shade of inde-
cision in the mind of any one of these three
tall euphorbias. (Caper spurge).

The 'Roman Walk' in the morning,
when shadows fall, is almost picturesque.
There are some large clumps of Sysirinchium striatum in profuse bloom ; the
flower spikes and iris-like leaves are most
' showy,' contrasting well with the rocks
and rounded masses of leaf and flower near

them.   The little pale yellow flowers,
taken singly, may seem rather insignificant,
yet there is something moving almost, in
their religious attention to the hour which
unwritten laws have determined ; for even
when gathered and kept in water in the
house, at a distance from the windows,
they shut up just the same, punctual to
a minute.   Lovely little purple Linaria
reticulata (aureo-purpurea) scatters itself,
self-sown, about the ledges, with the sweet
sad-coloured night stock ; and I am afraid
we tread heavier than need be upon the
camomile, spread flatly·on the stony walk,
to make it give out all its aroma.   The
small campanula pulla's deep purple bells,
nod in crevices near edelweiss clothed in
grey cottony bloom.   It is curious to see the
horror which an English dweller in Switzerland feels for this throned queen of alpine
flowers !   That edelweiss, a name *we* pro-
nounce almost with reverence, should
ever be called 'a cockney flower,' seems
almost past belief.   Yet so it is, and I am
sorry, for there had been a certain pride
when I thought our plants were finer on

the heights of the rock-garden, than in its lower ranges! There is mesembryanthemum and painted portulaca, a coral schizostylis, a yellow sysirinchium, and the stonecrops are coming into bloom. The artichoke rears itself grandly, almost like some grey-leaved giant fern, on the top ridge of rock, casting a great shadow across the stones.

A broad border—screened from a stray bit of kitchen garden by a battlemented arbor-vitæ hedge—has been divided into large squares of favourite plants. There is a square of ranunculus, and this is a disappointment. I believe the flower resents its removal from the old place under the south wall. Our ranunculus used to be small fireballs of vermillion and gold. Then there is a square of yellow sweet sultan, and with it a lovely lily with sea-green silvery leaves. Pancratium maritimum is the right name, I believe, but I prefer to call it a Star Lily. There are carnations, and then most delicately beautiful Spanish iris; a large flowered variety. The last square in the border is a blue mass of anchusa, not Italica, but the native wild sort.

The air just there is perfumed with musk. We let the musk wander at will all over this border. We give it neither care nor culture, and it gives back to us, for nothing, the treasure of its sweetness. With the parterre which lights up the lawn before the dining-room windows, I have little to do. The Gardener plans the colours and arrangement of it, and I feel it is in good hands; two centre beds this season appear to me especially happy. They are the white Bride gladiolus, mixed with deep red Tuscan rose; pure white and crimson.

The other long-shaped, narrow parterre we have tried to pattern out like one I saw last summer on a sunny Somerset rectory terrace. It was in vandykes of many-coloured verbena; ours is chiefly variegated and scarlet pelargonium, blue lobelias, both bronze, leaved and green, dwarf ageratum—tagetes, for yellow, and serastium tomentosum, known sometimes as Summer Snow. This snow looks very brilliant from a distance, seen through openings in the dark yew hedge. White is perhaps too much neglected in the ordering of coloured plots ; yet in all the best art of old times, in stained glass or eastern embroideries, it is the white parts that give brilliance to the whole. In the garden, yellow is the trouble. calceolarias I will not have ; I seek vainly some low-growing yellow, the same tone as the little double yellow rose that is teasing me by blooming high up out of reach by the garden gate. It should have the same effect, only in yellow, as the pink silene.

A short time since this Silene was used at Cliveden in a way that once seen, cannot be forgotten. An immense circle of pink, lay like a magic ring upon the grass. There is a set of jewel-shaped beds on a grand scale, leading up to it on either side. Between the ring and the lofty terrace, and the house, there simply lies unrolled, about a quarter of a mile of green velvet. Beyond the pink ring, dip down in sweetly wooded lines, steep cliffs and banks, to level meads, and windings of the silver Thames.

June 24.—On this midsummer morn St John's wort, under the Elms, is not yet in bloom. Yet I thought as I went over the garden, there could not be a more ideal 24th of June.

White and purple foxglove throng together in stately beauty in the Boccage and Fantaisie, with heads bent in the midday sun : but where one slender spike— milk-white or red—rises alone in some shady spot, peering through green brake fern, that, is better still ! I wonder what like was the 'lesser dusky foxglove,' observed by Gerard in John Tradescant's garden. Also his 'Digitalis ferruginea, with flower the colour of iron.' A fine plant of the yellow Swiss foxglove lives snug and solitary, under a currant bush in the kitchen garden. It is certainly handsome, but I never know whether to admire it much or not. There is always an uncertainty about the name of foxglove. In old French it is *Gante nostre dame ;* in high Dutch, as in German, *Finger-hut.*

And Roses !—It is roses, roses everywhere. A very Pasque della Rose. Never

do I remember the garden to be so much
of a real rose garden ; and the sweetest
rose of all is that which decks the sweet
brier hedge. Paul Nèron, with all his
seven inches across and no scent, is nothing to that little deep-pink brier rose !
The damask roses overspreading a corner
at the south wall are an ideal of rose loveliness. It is worth while to make a good
south place for this old rose ; it will soon
repay you a hundredfold in delicious
beauty. Once more, after nigh two score
years, I have the pleasure of smelling a
York and Lancaster rose. Her perfume
is divine. And we have a real black rose
(Empereur de Maroque ?), if gathered before the sun has time to burn it, most
beautiful—haunting the memory with that
old foolish rhyme—

> ' Rosy in the parlour, Rosy in the hall :
> Rosy was a black Rose, better than them all.'

As for our old blush rose, age does but
increase its charm.

JULY

VII

JULY

' This too will pass.'—*Persian Saying*.

JULY 3.—The thought of June-Roses would
have been marred had the grievous blight
that fell upon some of them been spoken
of at the time. Happily ours, which are
affected thus, are few, and the disfigure-
ment they suffer, slight compared with the
reports from other places. The roses
most dear to me have, however, suffered
most. The leaves of the Damask roses,
filling up that corner of the old south wall,
are white with blight; some of the York
and Lancasters the same, and the leaves
of some few other kinds are spotted all
over with brown. Not one of the Tea
roses is touched, nor any of our new
roses. Where the green leaves are

affected the flowers themselves also suffer, and look pale and stunted. Far worse than blight are the ravages of that cruel caterpillar which skins the leaves. He seems to prefer the old Blush rose to all others, and its leaves are the first to be attacked. I confess I hate the skinner, and destroy as many as I can lay my finger on. He is as wily as he is destructive, and being the same colour as the leaf is very hard to find. He has a way of lying close along the very edge of a leaf, or stretched out in such a position as to be almost indistinguishable from the veins. At mid-day, when the skinner has turned in under the leaf for shade, it is useless to hunt for he cannot possibly be seen. The best time for a successful massacre is in the morning, as early as you please. A little patch of fresher colour betrays a fresh-skinned portion of a leaf; there the enemy lies, invisible, except to the long-practised eye. As soon as he is discovered turn the leaf over and squeeze him tight ; there are grounds, however, for a dismal suspicion that unless the head be crushed the creature refills himself, the skin being tough, and next day he is at work again as hungry as ever. This suspected occurrence, however, I refrain from too closely verifying. The rose pest of former years—that little bright green caterpillar who after awhile sewed himself up in a leaf, became a tiny black chrysalis, and then emerged a smart little yellow moth, was not nearly so bad as the voracious Skinner. It is long since that little moth used to be too common in the garden. To see it again would at once bring back the past, with a feeling of dark summer evenings in long-lost years, and a pervading sense of the smell of rain upon the summer leaves.

There are some insects which would seem to be less abundant now than formerly. It gave me pleasure to meet a cockchafer one morning! The burnished rose-beetle who used to sit like a green jewel in the heart of a rose, or burr over the roses in the sunshine, I never see here now. Even the little leaf cutter bee has deserted us. His neatly rounded cuttings, sawn out of the rose leaves, disfigured them infinitely

H

less than one day's work of a skinner!
The musk rose that we planted last year is
flowering freely; small flowers with a small
delicious scent. I wonder if the delicate pink
of its petals is the 'musk-colour' of some
old writers! Does not Shakespeare write
somewhere of a 'musk-coloured coat?'

The white noisettes climbing all over
our old Stone Pine droop down to
the very grass in trails and wreaths
covered thick with bunches of little
white roses in lavish beauty. The curious strong fragrance fills all that end of
the garden. A child, a little elf of blue
eyes and pink cheeks running here and
there through and through the rose-falls,
was one day, like a vision from fairyland!
Rosa microphylla has grown herself into a
great green bush in the Fantaisie. But as
to flowering, she seems to think little of
that : two or three red flowers only, of no
account. The darlings of the year are the
great broad-flowered York and Lancasters.
I count them over morning after morning
as a miser counts his gold. It is worth a
visit just after sun-rise to see and smell

them with the dew upon their petals.
They are what Chaucer would call 'brode
roses,' so wide do their firm and well-set
petals spread. The white Cabbage—which
survives in borders skirting the older,
more distant shrubberies—is this summer
more than ever bounteous in its pure
white bloom. White Roses, however,
are not my favourites, excepting perhaps
Niphetos, the waxen Devoniensis and the
Japanese Rosa Rugosa.

There are summer days when it is too
hot for any but white flowers 'to deck the
house,' and in such sultry heat white
roses help to cool the shaded room. A
rose-de-meaux, a little perfumed nest of
prim pinkness, has bloomed like an old-
fashioned woodcut under the holly hedge.
I want to have near it the tiny Fairy rose
of former years, a wee bush pinked over
with the wee-est of China roses. Several
new plants of Souvenir d'un ami are
blooming well. No rose lasts so long
when gathered, as this does. The old
Maréchal Niel in the greenhouse has re-
newed his youth, and has given us his

hundreds this spring, while one planted under a north wall (according to advice) failed to do better for us than give a few greenish buds. The roses of the Boccage are superb in size and colour. The new ground suits them, and for half the day they are shaded by the elms. For a modern rose, I like Beauty of Waltham as well as any ; its form and luminous colour, emitting rays of crimson that almost 'bid the rash gazer wipe his eye,' are as perfect as any such rose can be. In the shade, behind the others, modestly blooms a lovely new rose, Madame Audot, scarcely differing, however, from our old friend the Maiden's Blush—perhaps a little richer in colour, and in scent a little poorer. It is pleasant to come suddenly upon this blaze of roses at a distance from the house, and divided from the nearer pleasaunce by grassy paths and lines of trees. So much for our Rose garden.   .   .   .

The garden is more fragrant this summer even than is its wont. One cannot tell which sweet scent does most prevail, whether that of sweet peas, or mignonette,

or honey-scented Alyssum; while about the iron gates in the old brick walls flexuosa honeysuckle flings perfume far and near. The sweet pea hedge round half the tennis-lawn is full of lovely caprices of colour. One set of white blossoms is tinged with pale bluish. That quaint, patchy, grayish and white kind, which by some absurd association of ideas, reminds me always of the old sign of the 'Bald-faced Stag' on Putney Heath, is frequent, and so is the old fashionedst of all —the pretty pink and white. We have not yet the new pink sweet pea, the colour of a moss rose or of raspberry cream. Plain white is, after all, the best perhaps. Nature never planned a lovelier flower of such airy lightness. It might shake its butterfly wings and fly, it is so lightly poised upon the slender stalk! Perhaps to the name 'sweet pea,' and to the sweet freshness of the flower, memories of childhood cling more closely than to any other garden name.

Sweet peas and mignonette should always grow together. Even the down-

trodden Everlasting pea ('Pease everlast-
ing,' and 'Save euerlasting,' as Gerard
calls them), with its large frank blossoms,
has this year won its way to favour.
That plant is in itself an epitome of all
the sermons of the year, with Courage
and Constancy for their text! It is as
good as a meditation by Jeremy Taylor.
We were very grave about it last year;
only a *very little* was to be permitted; it
was denounced as too encroaching; and a
quantity of it was ruthlessly cut away.
We believed its humiliation to be secure.
Not a bit of it! Never did it spread and
flourish and flower more abundantly than
it has done this summer. It ran round
the corner of the house and made a blooming bower of itself in the shade under the
east porch. It gave a rich deep pink
background for the white irises, and Blush
roses to the south; it actually climbed
up and looked in at the dining-room
windows, and nodded to us as we sat at
breakfast. 'J'y suis et j'y reste!' it said,
as plain as words; and after all I had
to confess its conquering beauty. The

Gardener would say I am rather weak about some things. 'pease everlasting,' has overcome ; and so has the white briony. I had said that this briony should not advance beyond a certain point. And I found myself to-day surrounded by the beauty of ten thousand ice-green blossoms, overspreading a low ivy wall, at least twelve feet beyond the bounds I had set. With unnumbered lengths of out-shot tendrils stretching all over it every way in eager quest for the touch of some sympathetic branch, with glossy ivy and blue berberis berries mixing through the flowers and foliage, it is certainly as people say, 'a picture.'

Near a little wicket gate at the end of a grass walk, grows a female briony, smaller and more reticent, wreathed about with round green fruit. During a short absence this was written to me—'No one has passed through the little green gate since you left, I am sure ; the briony has put out a tiny hand which clasps it so tight.' Totally different and most charming in its way, are the clumps of Alströmeria, whose orange

blossoms pass 'wrapt through many a rosy
change' into pink and white. It is in-
valuable in nosegays for the flower-glasses.
It will have to be transplanted from its
rather obscure corner at a distance from
the house by the garden-men's cottage.
It would keep the east border 'furnished'
until the time of phloxes. Ever since
mid-winter, the flower-glasses on our tables
have glowed with a rich succession of
Amaryllis formosissima and double scarlet
hibiscus. The long firm petals of this
amaryllis, well named 'the most beautiful,'
burn red beneath the silken surface—a just
imitation of old red enamel. I never tired
of watching the play of inner light ; the
turn of each petal shone like a piece of old
jeweller's work.

JULY 24.—One month has passed since
the garden lay flushed with the full glory of
midsummer. It is a little sad that nothing
now remains but a memory of it ; that
thinking of the garden flowers one must
say that this, and this, *has been !* Many
a flower since June has budded, bloomed,

and fallen ; and like the quickly passing sweetness of them, many a friend has come and gone. The dry, green paths hedged in with beech or rose are haunted in this parching weather, not alone by waving shadows on the grass, but by dear memories of a face or a voice that was here, and is not. The garden, through all its prime, was remarkable for its blue. Cloudy pillars of delphinium rose everywhere on the borders, showing well especially among the cryptomerias of the Fantaisie. There were many shades of blue, from pale sky to ultramarine. The dark blue double kind is a desirable plant, for its quality of lasting longer than its single sisters. Within the walls there grew a lovely group of white lily with pink roses against a misty background of blue larkspur, while on the other side the walk reigned in brilliant confusion, Himalayan poppies of every red and rosy tint. People say that these poppies, which we call Himalayan, or annual poppies, are common. Yet nobody seems to grow them ! They have been from May till now—to ourselves and every visitor—the wonder and joy of the garden. Whether double or single, like the field poppy they are full of a happy radiancy of colour which cheers both eyes and heart.

New combinations of colour and pattern are perpetually coming ; and I do not despair of the scarlets some day running into pure orange-yellow. There is a low-growing double kind, scarcely distinguishable from a pink carnation. There is one half-double with white petals hemmed with pink, and one streaked with crimson. The colours are all bright and clean, set off by the yellow stamens. One or two are rather handsome with black centres ; but these have none of the clear joyous grace of my favourites. For ' decking the house ' (to use again Parkinson's quaint phrase), they are admirable, lasting fresh for days, if gathered in the cool of morning. To me the petals are like fairy shells ; my housekeeper is reminded by them of the muslin gowns her grandmother used to wear.* The whole race of

* Our Himalayan poppies, having bloomed with

French poppies, so called, are far inferior, despite their grand seed vessels, and their fine grey foliage. . . . I am rebuked by the sweet face of one of these very poppies looking reproachfully at me across the table. The colour is vermillion-red and white, most delicate and pure. The seed of that poppy must be marked.

In the white splendour of their contrast to the poppies, how beautiful the blooming of Madonna lilies has been! (it is all 'has been,' now!) Does any one know why the lily *leaves* almost always fail? Before their buds flowered our lilies for the most part looked deplorable—their withered leaves hanging down around the tall stems. In due time, when the stems were crowned with the majesty beside which the glory of Solomon was as nought, we forgot the dreary deadness of the foliage. In Switzerland, where the cottage gardens are filled like those in England, with white lilies, I am told the stalk-leaves remain green. Two or three of our finest

us since 1872, have since become known as 'The Shirley Poppy!'

clumps failed suddenly—in one night, it seemed—the doomed plant withering down to the very bulb. This was an unusual disaster, and I blamed 'the invisible worm that flies in the dark and howling storm.' In the same border we have several great plants of Lilium auratum without a speck upon their leaves.

The Evening primrose (Œnothera) came into bloom before its appointed time, and her fair flowers are even larger than usual. Downy-winged moths hover round them in the dark warm evenings. It is said that those who watch may see the buds open. I have watched, but had never patience to wait long enough. Most flowers are best in the morning, when they are refreshed with dews and darkness; but to see Œnothera aright she 'must be visited by the pale moonlight,' when the air is still and heavy with the odours of night-scented flowers under the full golden moon of July. On such a dewless night, Œnothera expands her broad primrose flowers, and seems to throb through all her being with a strange moon-life. Once sown, the evening primrose takes care of itself ever after. We have them growing in a line along the Larch walk, all twined about and dressed with a large-blossomed wreathing pink convolvulus. Another company of them edging an evergreen border shine in the light of loveliness out of the sombre brown of cryptomerian darkness. Alas! Œnothera owns one fatal flaw. It is hard even to whisper of its repulsive smell—a smell which is also so sensitive that the flower seems to give it out or retain it at will. At night, if the stem be shaken, or if the flower-cup trembles at the touch of a moth as it alights, out pours the dreadful odour. I shall hope some day, for the perfumed white variety. Another old love of former years is the Indian moonflower. Some of the large white seeds were sent us in the winter from Madras, and now I am anxiously watching the growth of two fine plants which sprung from them. It used to blow at the end of July, when the moon was full, between 9 and 10 at night; opening wide, like a pure white convolvulus, with a delicious scent.

Night-blowing flowers are mostly pale or white. The nicotiana hanging on its stalk half-dead by day, is radiant as a silver star when night draws on. In the Boccage we have two fine clumps of spiderwort (Tradescantia), a flower I remember set amongst childhood's wonders, earliest almost of all flowers. Buds mass themselves in clusters all over the plants, and every day on each cluster appears a new three-cornered purple gem. The old fanciful likeness to spiders' legs can be but barely traced in the leaves. There is a sense of mysterious awe, in the way Gerard says the leaves are good ' for the bite of that Great Spider,' without naming the creature more particularly.

John Tradescant lived once at Dorney Court, not far from here. There is some tradition that there he presented his Pine-apple* to Charles II, and it is not many years since a little wayside public-house near, retained still the sign

* The first grown in England. At Dorney Court there is an old engraving, which represents Tradescant kneeling before the King in a garden, presenting his pine-apple.

of a Pine-apple. 'Deborah's' little mount in the parterre was a while ago parcel-gilt with the silver of small white hare-bells, and the gold of yellow stonecrop. It is grieving to recall thus the garden as it was! Sweet things do still remain, but after all the daily waterings—sometimes whole days are spent in watering—the place as a whole is parched up with long drought. Some things dwindle, and cannot by any means be saved. Eleven weeks without rain! Long weeks when the sun burns unclouded, and the only clouds are clouds of greenfly, that is the worst; greenfly that destroy whole rows of sweet peas in a single night, and blackfly that smother the fruit trees, and distort the stalks of lovely poppies. If one sits in the garden they settle all over one, and outside the garden, down along the roads, one encounters storms of flying aphides. Flycatchers sit stupidly on the rose arches, bewildered by the myriads that float in the air. The lime avenue is dried up, and yet dripping with honeydew. Rain will come at last, however, and meanwhile the trees will ripen their wood, and it may be that good will fall rather than harm, even to the green things that claim our pity now.

AUGUST

VIII

AUGUST

' Such virtue have my marigolds,
  Within their stalks enfolde,
That Phœbus with his burning beames
Cannot their leaves unfolde.

' The double daisies all in rankes
    About my garden goe,
With comelie course of camamile
    That spreadeth to and fro.'

Hugh Plat, 1572.

AUGUST 18.—How full of charm is the return after absence to a beloved garden ! One comes home rejoicing, to see with a fresh eye each dear tree and each familiar spot of lawn or border, and bringing home stores of pleasant memories with sweet suggestions for new delights to perfect and bring to pass and make one's own another day.

I note for special use these :—A Mande-

villia growing in the open air. It covers
half the front of an old house, climbing up
to the roof, and when I saw it the pure
white blossoms were clustered thickly all
over it. The situation in which this
Mandevillia grows and has flourished for
many years is warm and sheltered, the
house-walls of hummel-stone, being built
in a niche under a limestone cliff. Possibly this may not be the only greenhouse
creeper that might thrive in the open air,
at least during the summer months. We
have tried successfully the white and the
salmon-coloured black-eyed Thunbergia ;
also convolvulus from Indian seed, which
has richer and more varied colouring than
the common convolvulus major.

The lightness and gaiety of a flowery
hedge of it is indescribable. That which
I saw is nearly 10 feet high, the frame-
work made of crossed stakes, the convolvulus climbing and twining up to the top
and flowering profusely on both sides.

Espaliers of gooseberries I also saw
at an old place in Hampshire, bordering
the walks round three sides of the kitchen-

garden. Nothing can be more neat and useful than these espaliers, the goose-berries being easily gathered without much prickling by thorns, while nets fall comfort-ably over, protecting them from the birds. It was a delightful garden ! A long green walk lay between rows of hollyhocks, pink, black, white, and pale primrose. These lovely hollyhocks had the free, aspiring form, that is now so rarely seen when the blossoms seem to clump irregularly up the slender stem. Roses and most of the summer flowers had faded from the borders at the time of my visit. White everlast-ing pea—and red, strongly scented, fraxi-nella were among the few that still bloomed in beauty. A favourite plant of red fraxinella was lost from our garden a year or two ago, and I had not seen one since. The scent of the flower is said to be due to the emission of a vapour that can be set on fire with a lighted match. That, must one day be tried. One has but to pass a glove lightly across the flower, however, and it is perfumed all over. In another part of that old garden grew white strawberries of a peculiar kind. They flower and fruit at the same time, and the fruit, which is in flavour like a Hautbois, goes on ripening as late as October or November. Every little runner bears its flowers and straw-berries. A basketful of ripe berries was gathered the day that I was there—August 10. I believe in Shakespeare's time straw-berries were still called 'straeberries,' from the Saxon 'strae' or 'stray,' indicating the habit of the strawberry in putting forth runners to a distance from the parent plant, giving to both independent life. In some outland country places they still talk of the 'straeberry.'

In a beautiful sea garden, high above the sea, half hid in groves of ilex, a spot so sheltered that even in winter the lawns are scarcely ever swept by the wild sea winds, I found the little white sweet-scented* orchis in the middle of the month, growing on the brown parched-up turf. There had been no rain there, nor hardly any dew ; the lawns, destitute of any poor vestiges of verdure, lay 'gasp-

* Commonly called ' Lady's tresses,' or ' traces.'

ing as a thirsty land.' Yet here and there,
made bold by the idleness of scythe and
mowers, suddenly arose these green and
white points of orchis. One of them, as
it seemed in one night, shot up 4 inches,
and this one I took home with me. It is
set in water by my window, and now I can
watch the untwisting of the plaited tress,
as day by day its smoothness roughens
with twin - petalled moonlight - coloured
flowers. It was a pretty notion to liken
the little flower-spike to tresses of the
Virgin's hair, though one may perhaps
just fancifully trace in it a mingling of
pagan fairyism ; for mermaidens combed
their sea-green locks, and I myself once
knew the traditional fairy lady of a well,
all in green, with long green hair. Her
well-spring bubbled up by the side of a
deep West Country lane, and many children and old people have seen the green
fairy rise at twilight from the water !

The House,* whose high windows and
turrets look down over these brown lawns

* Highcliff, Hampshire. Belonged at that time to
Louisa, Lady Waterford.

and flowers, and ilex woods, is romantic;
like a poet's dream, rather than a house
of the nineteenth century. Its stones,
however, are the grey stones of an old
house in Normandy. They were brought
over many years ago, and rebuilt here on
the edge of the sea in strange architecture,
with the carved mouldings and gargoyles,
and oriel windows of the past, put in just
as they were. The open parapet round
the roof reads thus in stone letters :—
'*Suave mari magno turbantibus æquora
ventis Terra magnum alterius spectare lab-
orem.*' The words seem to make music
with the soft measure of the waves below,
and the sound of the wandering winds.
The thick-leaved ilexes soon loose themselves in woods of chestnut and fir, and
paths cut through them in lines of endless
shade close in at last, each with an arch
of sapphire sea. Beyond the edges of the
woods, wild honeysuckle and low sea-
blown oaks, and brambles, grow together
in a sweet entanglement, and grassy paths
between are set with purple heather and
knapweed (knops, or hardheads), and

yellow Fleabane ; and here a legion of butterflies perpetually dance and play, and make merry in the sunny weather. It should make amends for much sorrow in the world of Nature to see these thousands of beautiful creatures, secure and happy in their innocent joy.

Along this green glade your feet are every moment ensnared by long-reaching brambles, and every step disperses a fluttering cloud of butterflies. They are so tame that scarcely will they rise at your approach, often giving the observer time to stoop and examine with a lens their spangled wings and silver-topped antennæ and busy proboscis. The Fleabane is the butterflies' dear delight. (Did not the child who called them ' flutterbyes ' hit upon a better name ?) Two or three of diverse kinds will often prank their wings, and unrolling long black tongues, dig for honey settled together on the same flower, though flowers may not be few; but when a Painted lady (Vanessa cardui), and a silver-spotted Fritillary meet on one flower they are sure to fall out, and rising chase each other hotly. Besides the multitudes, of common and uncommon white butter-flies and little cloudlets of the azure-winged Alexis, Peacocks, and Tortoiseshells, and Painted ladies in troops with now and then a rarer clouded yellow Colias, or rapid Fritillary, disport themselves up and down the glade till past mid-day. Long may their happy world be unknown to green gauze nets and murderous ammonia bottles! I am curious to know if any variation has ever been observed in the markings of the wings of these insects. I have for years closely examined Peacocks and Tortoise-shells and Atalantas, and can never find the colours or patterns to vary in the least degree from those of the oldest specimens I can remember. In the glade dragon-flies dart fiercely to and fro, and wild ' bees are busy on their threshold old.' The honey gathered on that Hampshire coast is crystal pale this summer. It was made, as I was told, from fruit tree blossoms in the spring, the long-continued drought having dried up every drop of honey in the heather-bells.

Magnolia Grandiflora

IX

HOME AGAIN !

'Nature always wears the colours of the spirit.'

AND now I have been tasting the pleasures of roaming through my own principality once more!—noting with the keenest zest the changes that eighteen days have wrought. I want to go all over it again. In a grand red glow, covering an area of 462 square feet of lawn, lighting up the old hall and the windows of other rooms that look that way, like the reflex of some fine sunrise, just beyond the south porch, lies the Sumach tree (Rhus cotinus). I cannot say that it stands upon the lawn, as would be said of any other tree, for the beautiful soft masses of it are like nothing else but those great white cumuli, or summer storm-clouds, steeped in a crimson after-glow, when we watch their changeless glory moving slowly on, upon the low horizon. These sumach snows however, are reddened by hot weeks of

July suns ; they cover all the tree, till gently they shimmer down and lie still upon the turf. Not a branch or a twig, scarcely even one green leaf, strays out amid the lightness of these plumes of marabout to break their dim monotony. This plumage of the tree is sunny red, cooled with grey or lilac shadows. Ever since June has it been ripening into this miracle of misty beauty. The lawns are burnt, but the parterre is formal and brilliant just as it should be. So are the zig-zags of verbena and Pelargoniums beyond the yew hedges. The southern wall is fragrantly overhung with festooned clematis. But all these are quickly passed by. I long to know all's well with the Fantaisie and the Boccage. Ah ! the sweet pea hedge round the tennis-lawn is gone and past. Turn - cap Lilies, proudly splendid, replace the roses of the Fantaisie. The cryptomeria elegans, intermingling here with verdure of wonderful freshness, seem to rejoice in the dry weather, and fair flowers of deep blue salvia begin to blow.

Three paces through the deep shadow of 'the wood,' and there is the broad border of the Boccage in all its glory! To know how this had fared in my absence, while yet the ground had not received comfort from any kindly rain, had been my secret trouble. I should like for the moment to be some one else, and as a stranger to describe this border quite impartially! Yet the only words I can devise as some one else's first impression seem cold and dry. Such as 'a beautiful band of flowers, that reflects the highest credit on the care and skill which have made it what it is.' That will not do. I must be myself, and try to give some faint outline of it. When I saw it last—last month— roses and pinks were over; and besides some budding corn-flags and hyacinthus candicans, there was little to give grace to the border, saving certain patches and rounds and clumps of green traced in and out between the roses. I returned to find this young green grown out of all knowledge, and flowering with a strange luxuriance of bloom, the flowers all mixing

in delicious confusion. There is Ladies'
Pincushion (Saudades), made in pale coral,
passing through velvet shades of red to
deep 'murrey,' stuck with silver pins as
usual. Lobelia fulgens (the Cardinal's
flower), burn between the tufts of white
and lilac Sultan's flower (Sweet Sultan).
Gaillardia picta Lorenziana mingles with
Gailliardia picta flowering in gold and
crimson petals, fantastically nicked, set
round in little coronets; a bunch or two
of lilac Catananche, deep lengths of Marvel
of Peru in three bright colours, many
coloured China asters, double stocks,
lupins, dwarf phloxes, one choice corner
filled in with salpiglossis of richly varied
colours, brown, purple, and grey. Sword
lilies flash scarlet here and there amid
all these, and grandest of all are the
fine plants of hyacinthus candicans, each
plant sending up three or four great stems,
blue-green with the bloom of health, and
each bearing a ring of bells in ivory-white.
A white 'Peach-leaf bell flower,' (campanula) in a shadowy place near at hand betrays
by contrast the only failure amid the perfect

K

beauty of these fine hyacinthus flowers—
failure in the purity of their whiteness.

Against a low beech hedge at the back
there is a stately line of auratum lilies,
counting seventy-three great heads of
bloom with store of buds rich in promise
for weeks far into the autumn. And
around the lilies are enlaced large African
marigolds of lemon and deep gold colour,
with scattered posies of little striped
French marigolds and of Zinnia Haageana.
At the farthest end a thicket of dianthus
superbus scents half the garden, and nearest
to the Fantaisie, a narrow grass walk in-
tersecting the border and leading into
Glorietta is fringed with lobelia sene-
cioides luxuriantly green, and most delicately blue. Chrysanthemum tricolor fills
up the corner, and on the other side deep
purple and blue perennial-blooming pansies
set off the clean yellow rays and chocolate
eyes of Rudbeckia Newmannia. Towering
above the junipers tall 'flowers of the
Sun' keep watch, their green buds not
opened yet. Mignonette and honied alyssum and orange and red tigridias seem to

grow naturally in and out between the
other plants, with now and then a sharp
gleam of roses in second bloom. How
obscure and dull is the thought-picture,
the best I can make of the Boccage border!
Old Parkinson would paint it in a dozen
words! He would just say, 'the place is
like a piece of tapestry of many glorious
colours to increase every one's delight.'
Yet the colour is not all. A pervading
perfume works like a charm about the
place to bind in one sweet whole the outward brightness of the flowers, and the
unseen soul of them, which is their scent.

I wonder how many moles there may
be in the garden. The Gardener certainly
would borrow Keats's phrase, and echo
heartily 'the demon mole!' For they
burrow and throw up their earthworks,
and overturn stones, and uproot precious
plants, caring nothing for right or wrong.
For me, the mole is simply 'the four-
handed mole,' the odd little persecuted
wild beast (one of the last left in England),
the little velvet-coated gentleman-navvy,
who excavates in darkness, carrying his

subways across our neatest turf-walks without the least regard to propriety or order in the garden. At the entrance of the Fantaisie, indeed, for the last twelve years a mole-run has existed across the path. Our attempts to stop this right of way have signally failed. Scores of moles were caught year after year, and gibbeted near the spot as a warning, till at last the order came for executions to cease. I could no longer endure the piteous sight of the beautiful mole-skin coat squeezed round the middle, and the two ungainly serviceable hands that had worked so hard, helplessly spread on either side. So the underground ' taupies'' pertinacity scored that time ! and the run remains to this day. Long ago, when the world was young, mole-hills were thought to be useful for lambs to sit upon, or to shelter under if the wind blew cold. ('Nootie-stumps,' they call them in Gloucestershire.) Lately, however, it has been discovered that 'there is nothing more useful to the floriculturist, whether for pots or borders, than earth from a mole-hill ; ' for, 'as the mole lives entirely on worms and insect larvæ which are found in the best soil, that which he throws to the surface while in pursuit of his prey, finely pulverised, and free from the seeds of weeds as it will be found to be, is just in the state for producing the best flowers.'

A long-desired white Tigridia has just now for me all the charm of a new possession. The cream-white flowers, with crimson-spotted centres, are a most exquisite delight. It is one of those strange beings which look as if they had come from another world. Until now, the two tigridias — the yellow and the red with their threefold flowers—seemed always incomplete. Now, nothing more is needed. I do not want a blue or a pink tigridia ; this mysterious white third is enough.

SEPTEMBER

X

SEPTEMBER

' All tendrils green of every form and hue,
  Together intertwined and trammell'd fresh :
  The vine of glossy sprout ; the ivy mesh,
  Shading its Ethiop berries ; and woodbine,
  Of velvet leaves and bugle-blooms divine ;
  Convolvus in streaked vases flush ;
  The creeper, mellowing for an autumn blush,
  And virgin's bower, trailing airily ;—

J. Keats.

SEPTEMBER 1.—The soft triumph of the Sumach is over. According to the supreme beauty of her prime, is now her forlorn and wretched ruin. All in a day, so it seemed, the feathery fluff began to crisp and loosen. One night the west wind blew in his strength, and left our Wig tree well-nigh bald. The marabout plumes, blown hither and thither, accumulated in angles of the house, and all the borders thereabouts were bedded deep in fluffy pink. But even this relic of grace is past, and the tree, nearly un-leaved (for her feathers left no room for leaf), all dishevelled and hung with rags and tatters, is an almost ghastly sarcasm on her summer self.

Sunday, September 13.—Autumn or spring ! 'I know not which is sweetest, no, not I'—the deep mellow calm of an evening such as this, in the middle of September, or the green brilliance of the spring. The tone is rich, like the colour of an old Venetian master; and how sad ! with the strange sweet sadness of all last things—last days, last hours. The air is filled with a golden warmth, and all tremulous with the sound of bells. The chimes of four churches make music to-gether, within a half circle of four miles. Save for the dazzling glow of tall crimson phloxes, or where the leaf of some Virginian vine, impatient of the lingering summer breaks into sudden scarlet, or where great Sunflowers burn in fair majesty serene, the tones of colouring are subdued and solemn; the young moon alone shines coldly through thin saffron clouds that pass across the far azure of the southern sky, while in the west a pink flush, deepening into orange fires, reflects back rosy-gold upon the lulled earth beneath. Across the petunias and many-coloured zinnias * bend fruitful branches of apple and of pear. There is a sense of settled calm and peace, of home, and of all that may be most pleasureful and most secure, in these plenteous boughs weighed down by the load of their good, great apples, and gently swelling pears, and the mellow round of each ripening fruit glows as if illumined from within. And now a great silence steals on upon the air. The bells have ceased, their last vibrations lost along the far-spread fields. The sharp ' tzit, tzit,' of a robin, or a beetle's drone in passing flight, seem but to intensify the stillness. In this beautiful hour, as twilight deepens down upon the flowers, they seem to open their hearts to you and speak.

* 'Where are we to put the zenanas?' asked a friend's old Scotch gardener t'other day !

The cold half-withdrawn look of common day has vanished from each lovely face, and as you pass by, voiceless, they tell you sweet nothings without words.

It is more strange than perhaps at first sight appears,—the illumination of flowers and bright coloured objects after sundown, while the green of surrounding grass and foliage is lit only with a sombre radiance. I may be pardoned for giving a suggested theory in explanation, thus : The colour of all objects depends upon the kind of illumination they receive. A completely yellow light thrown upon a nosegay will kill all colour excepting in the yellow flowers. Newton discovered that sunshine and all white lights have the power of pouring every conceivable shade of colour upon all objects, and these again have the power of extinguishing all shades except the few which suit their own substances and textures. 'A blue salvia extinguishes all the red, yellow, green, and possibly the violet rays, while a red poppy absorbs all the violet, blue, green, and possibly yellow. We therefore see the latter brilliantly red, and the former purely blue.' When mellowed fruits and yellow and red flowers shine at evening it is because the sunset light comes to them through more and more of the air that envelopes the earth, and which though invisible, quenches almost entirely the violet, blue, and green. All objects disposed towards yellow and red are then illuminated as with a pure light of these two colours, and they gleam out triumphantly, because all other green, blue, and violet objects are more or less deprived of their favourite rays. Nothing of this, however, quite explains why white and yellow flowers often appear so bright at night, or why some other flowers—and notably some kinds of crimson snapdragon (antirrhinum)—do often shine, so as to attract the eye from a distance on some very dull grey days. These (as indeed all flowers in some degree) doubt less have a self-luminous power, which we call phosphorescence, whatever that may be.

We have already had large store of delicious, well-sunned wall fruit—peaches,

figs, and plums.   I can believe that, had
we means to build and keep up long
ranges of houses — peach houses, and
nectarine and fig-houses—they would be
built, and we should draw from their rich
produce the same enjoyment in the same
way that others do who possess glass.
But I do not believe that these houses
would ever give me the same delight as
does the little basketful of fruit and flowers
that I find placed on my table every morning on these late summer days.   I do not
believe that the finest fruit ripened under
glass could compare at all with the beautiful red sun-ripened peaches, picked from
the old brick walls ! My basketful holds
sometimes one such perfect peach, two or
three purple figs, yellow plums bursting
with sugared juice; or a golden pear, a few
Muscat or Madresfield Court grapes lovely
in their exquisite bloom of misty gold or
black, while single flowers of richly-scented
tuberose and dainty pink begonias lie
intermixed with the green vine leaves
and the fruits. Our sole pride of glass
fruit culture is in the vinery.   Season

after season our grapes excel in size and in flavour. The Muscats remind me of the grapes of Italy. Travelling along the Corniche in days before railroads, grapes, large and golden-green as these are, the peasant people would bring to us and pour into our laps, with green figs and china roses all fresh and dewy. The quantity of immense bunches that are gathered out of our one small house, lasting up to nearly Christmas, never fails to be a surprise to me, although it is always the same every year.

OCTOBER

L

XI

OCTOBER

'Withered leaves, one—two—and three—

.   .   .   .   .   .

Through the calm and frosty air
Of this morning bright and fair
Eddying round and round they sink
Softly, slowly.'

W. Wordsworth.

OCTOBER 19.—My best yellow autumn window curtains are up! No other curtains could ever please me so much as these. But to make it understood how perfect in their way they are, the windows also must be described. They are almost the only windows in the house that are not old-fashioned casements. At that period, in the beginning of the century, when in most old houses the picturesque and small-paned casements were made into sash-windows, the windows of the room

I inhabit were enlarged and modernised. Here then, are two very large sash windows, their aspect almost due south, with the large frames and dull bald character usual to such windows. Ugly as they are, they were never altered, for the sake of the fine wide opening made when the sash is thrown up. Covering the entire space of the upper half, and enframing the whole, hang my curtains: green for summer, and in autumn, golden yellow. The pair is odd, for there must be nothing commonplace about the room! so the one is magnolia, the other chiefly vine. On the right is a bold intricate pattern of glossy leaves with perhaps a great white creamy blossom— a chalice of so rich a scent—set here or there upon the branches, with blue sky between. The left is all vine, made admirably to suit the seasons. In winter the curtain is drawn back, as it were; for a few interlacing barren lines keep out no light. The thin delicate arabesque of spring gives place to summer, when the green comes full and cool and shades the noonday sunlight. And now in

autumn, my left-hand curtain is all yellow
gold, reflecting back gold sunshine of its
own.   There should be dispersed amid the
gold, bunches of ripe green grapes, like
clustered berylls.   That part of the orna-
mental needlework I has not been well done
this year, and the grapes are mostly shrunk
and mildewed.   To repair the loss of them
slender jasmine twigs set round with
narrow dark green leaves, hold out little
silver stars, peering round the corners,
stretching round the window-sills, while
across them comes a dash of red Virginian
climber.   The one fault I find, is that my
yellow curtains do not endure.   Come a
sharp frost, or strong gust of wind—they
are gone in a moment.

The failure of the grapes is this year a
serious disappointment to the birds, who
count upon their vintage at the windows;
yet the shutters opening in the morning
discover them some times at work.   There
is a blackbird, with full black chest,
swallowing the grapes as fast as his golden
bill can manage it; or a thrush sits in the
Vine taking breath between his mouthfuls,

while the sun shines sidelong on his spotted breast; or a robin shows his red waistcoat for a moment. He is not, I fear, my robin that has hitherto been so constant to the window—for twelve months past he has hardly missed a day. Bold and familiar in the winter, silent and hurried at nesting time—not a feather in his tail, and very shy, when moulting. Gay and *insouciant* in his new suit, looking as big again, and trilling half a bar at a time short and full, but 'always regular to his meals' at the saucer of sopped biscuit. Dear little tame robin! I shall grieve if he is dead; but I think he will come back in the winter, when birds are hungry. They say that robins go to the seaside in October; and another saying would have the young birds kill the old ones at this season. Even this is better than the way my friends the swallows behave. Up to the time when they all left England— about the 13th—they seem to have been still occupied with late broods of young. It was indeed without my consent that they thus foolishly employed themselves here in the north porch. If they could but have understood, I should have persuaded them to stay a little longer, to give their young a chance. On the 16th only one swallow was seen, and three days after a tragedy happened in the porch! Late in the afternoon a poor little full-fledged swallow lay dead on the cold stones. The forsaken nestling may have fallen in its hungry efforts for food, or have attempted in its weakness to follow the stronged-winged parents, whose cruel desertion it is hard to forgive. Strange and inexplicable is the migratory instinct with birds. It is then, more powerful with them than even mother's love? and yet love is said to be stronger than death.

The habits of the swallows who make themselves at home in our entrances, north and south, are full of interest. The red-throated chimney swallows like best the north. On the south side are martins. Both kinds agree in departing from ancestral laws in their ways of house building. The typical swallow's nest used formerly to be neatly built up—usually under the eaves—with a hole for them to fly in and out. Our swallows of to-day make flat hasty nests on projecting ledges inside the porch. One nest (re-filled three times last summer) is made up of ugly blackish clay, bearded with long straws of hay hanging down. Is it not a new thing for swallows to build with hay? We have only one really well-rounded neatly-finished nest, and this is a martin's. The chimney swallows seem to be most hurried and careless. One of our families makes no nest at all, there is simply a layer of mud laid on the ledge. Along the rim the five newly feathered young ones sit in a row to be fed, like five little old owls in miniature. There is one thing that a swallow never forgets or forgives, and that is destroying the old nests. The place remains empty to this day where once we cleared away two overcrowded nests. They love overcrowding. I watched the old birds—on their return the following May—inspect the place, flying in and out and round about it; but either they forsook us altogether, or nested elsewhere about the house.

Flowers still are blooming everywhere in the garden. There are still beautiful red roses, smelling as sweet as June. Rosa rugosa has only just ceased to flower. A great clump of pale blush anemone japonica at the south end of the broad walk has flowered grandly for some time past. A clump of white ones from the kitchen garden is to be planted there also, since it is plain that they look best in large masses. Had we room I should like to plant blue salvia next to the white anemones. The fine blue of this old salvia enriches now the whole garden in almost every part. The colour is said by some to be in a false key, and as such to be out of tune with the more natural greens and blues around, contrasting ill with the lovely tones of nemophila or of the blue daisy— or even with the firmament itself! I know not how this may be, but to me it is nevertheless a magnificent blue—nearest, perhaps, in tone to the deep blue of the alpine gentian, and losing beside the gentian only because it lacks its depth of jetty heart. Pure ultramarine must be used in the painting of either flower. Our old walls are all well-furnished with the vivid orange-scarlet glow of tropæolum. It gives promise, too, of lasting on as long as winter frosts delay. I cannot give the name of this special variety of Tropæolum, or nasturtium is it? Its leaf is bluish and round, and the plant seems to be always in flower, from August until far into November.

In the entrance court the old use-less green gages and golden drop plum trees against the walls are dressed out in these gay flowers, climbing, streaming, creeping, clustering about all over them, branch and stem. The vivid colouring is splendid; it seems but a few days since it mixed in many places with the purple of Jackman's clematis. At this moment the blossoms intermingle here and there with tall, yellow helianthus. The aged fruit trees are doomed, and flowering climbers are to cover the walls in their place. The standard cherry tree between the pyramid yews is to be cut down, and a broader flower border to be made. It is hard to sentence the cherry tree! In spring it is so like a great round nosegay of loveliest blossom, and when the cherries begin to redden a thrush so loves to build its nest in it, and at evening to perch on the top and sing the lingering day away. Yet the cherry tree must go. These kind of changes which at intervals have to be made throughout the garden cause us a thousand regrets. When the young trees and shrubs thrive and grow all round as Nature intended, the very success and growth of them overturns all our plans, and changes are inevitable. 'The Fantaisie' has changed its character and is not the same in any way as it was when first laid out. Then, flowers and evergreen shrubs grew together on either side the turf walk, and each enhanced the other's charm. Twelve or thirteen years later the cryptomerias and aucubas and berberis have grown so large, that nearly all the flowers are crowded out, and a new aspect takes possession of the whole. The law of change which thus rules the garden has lately forced us to remove a large English yew from the spot which it has occupied for many years. It was pushing its dark growth right into the beautiful grey foliage of an Abies amabilis. So last month the grand move had to be arranged.

To watch the transplanting of a tree is a choice amusement of autumn in the garden. The work begins early in the morning. Two, three, four hours or more, according to the size of the tree, is taken up with digging round and throwing out the earth. The roots and rootlets have to be carefully separated : not cut or severed more than is necessary. The tree is tied close with strong cords : all its lower branches bound up together. The head gardener watches and gives his orders quietly, jumps down into the trench, and lends a hand himself with spade or pick : walking round, returning again and again. Silently, cheerfully, the men work. A wholesome fragrance of new earth spreads upwards in the air. The labour is severe, but at last the tree stands free, with a great

Starry Stitchwort

ball of earth round his roots. The bell goes for the men's dinner; powdered all over with brown mould they scramble up and shake themselves, throw an old mat over the roots, and depart for their hour of rest. The men return refreshed, and set to work again with a will; and now three tall stout poles, the ends meeting at top in a triangle, are set up and fixed, with ropes and pulleys fastened to them. It may take long to adjust all right, but at last the tree swings high in the air, dangling from the summit of the triangle. The excitement of the moment grows intense. Two or three men in the pit below steady and guide the ascending mass; four or five pull the ropes with might and main. The tree swings fair above the centre of a trolley, wheeled up to the edge ready to receive it. The Gardener holds on to the strong shaft or handle of the trolley, his eye fixed anxiously on the swaying tree, encouraging the men, directing every movement. The ropes are tight; the tree is well up. 'Now let go! slacken the ropes!—gently—so!' Gently the tree is lowered down upon the platform of the trolley, and the ball of earth once more is wrapt in mats.

Now begins the dragging, and pushing, and pulling; there's a shove and a tug all together, and the tree is fairly off on its journey. Toiling along the gravel-walks, the triumphal car rolls slowly on. The progress may be short or long; somewhere it ends, at the edge of a big hole prepared in the special spot designated to receive the tree. Soon he slides safely down into the bed ready made in the hole. There is a merry shovelling in and stamping of the earth, leaving a little ditch all round to hold the great watering which is the ending of the work; and there the tree is left, looking as if he had been there all his life. Unmoved the neighbouring trees and shrubs stand round, and not a green leaf flutters welcome to the new-comer; it is henceforth as if the transplanted tree had never been anywhere else. Should the tree we have to move be larger than usual, it may take to do it twenty-six working hours or more.

Men of old time planted trees for pos-
terity. With far-seeing wisdom they
planned many a stately avenue, which
still remain the ornament and pride of our
fine old country houses. We do not in
these days seem always to look so far
beyond the present. When a few years
ago I planted a row of young limes (in
old books they are 'lines') as a continua-
tion of the lime avenue, with arbor-vitæ
between each tree, and parellel to these a
double row of larch, and a beech hedge
along the walk between the limes and the
larch—I did not foresee the dilemma that
has ensued. A decision must before long
be made between the selfish enjoyment of
the present, extending perhaps to a few
uncertain years, or the future and lasting
improvement of· the place, which I shall
not see. While we hesitate the trees grow
on. The stems of the limes grow thick
and smooth, and their branches spread ;
the beautiful green arbor-vitæ flourish,
and are rapidly making handsome trees ;
my favourite larch send up strong tall
shoots every season threatening to over-

whelm everything; while the beech
hedge is so luxuriant that I am tempted
to sacrifice all to it.   Which is it to be?

'WHY should we sorrow,
  That summer's dazzling ray
  So soon has passed away?
  Whilst we can borrow,
  From Autumn's yellow light
  A scene more purely bright?

'Where'er the eye can wander,
  The garden and the field,
  A richer prospect yield.
  Earth seems to squander
  Her plenty in the sheaf
  Her gold in ev'ry leaf.'

NOVEMBER

XII

NOVEMBER

' Change and decay in all around I see,
O Thou who changest not abide with me.'

J. Newman.

' The spirit culls
Unfaded amaranth, when wild it strays
Through the old garden ground of boyish days.'

J. Keats.

NOVEMBER 30, 1887.—November is going
out with all the soft warmth of a summer
month. On such a day as this, the gum
cistus gives out its sweetness, and the
aroma of its leaves floats past upon the
milk-warm wind. I found to-day upon
a grass walk a wind-snapt branch of it,
and holding it in my hand as I walked,
the garden seemed all wrapt in delicious
airs as from some sweet southern clime.
There are roses too : real pink roses in

the garden, full blown, and full of summer fragrance.   And tea-roses are showing large firm swelling buds which look as if come what might, they were resolved to open.   Little white blossoms shine amongst the wood strawberry leaves under the south windows.   Ferns still are freshly green : only here and there they are changing colour in groups of orange, russet-brown and gold.   Growing among the 'rocks' on the Roman Walk, a plant of yellow Sysirhinchium which has flowered persistently during the past six months, still points with primrose yellow its narrow reed-like leaves.   The glory of the garden is the Christmas rose.   Our one great healthy clump is, in the heart of it, silvered all over with the promise of finer bloom than it has ever been known to show.   It means to bloom rather earlier than usual this season, and as yet has no bower of fir branches built over it to ward off the frost.   Scarcely the least tinge of red in any one of the score of well opened blossoms mars as yet their perfect white.

Beautiful as they are, we do not often gather them for the house, for when parted from their own dark foliage, Christmas roses lose always a part of their life and spirit ; and yet the leaves look too coarse when cut, and besides being difficult to arrange, to cut them off from the plant will often seriously wound it. I have tried to arrange with them sprays of flexiosa honeysuckle embrowned with winter, but nothing really answers. Chrysanthemums on the other hand, seem made for 'decking up the house' just now ! They are brilliant in white and yellow and chocolate brown and all the indescribable tints we know and love so well. But our dear Christmas roses are best left among the dead leaves, growing in the earth where they love to be, and there they gladden our eyes with un-looked - for joy, when summer's flight makes the heart sad. The purple coloured and green Hellebores that were sent us from the north, hardly do their best here. They are budding well, but they are rather unwilling denizens, and wear the look of existing here only as specimens. Notwithstanding the unusual warmth, the garden in these late November days is dull and sorrowful. Broken, blackened wrecks of past delight, strewed over every part of it, seem to impart a more than common gloom. The sense of 'change and decay,' pervades the very air about us, as we traverse the garden paths, along by the ruined shrubberies and borders, or pass near haunted, grassy ways.

There is always a certain charm in the curious mosaic of autumn leaves, lying as they fall, this way and that, across each other on every side. Leaves are mostly sure to fall picturesquely, and to die off in fine shades of brown and tawny red. And yet, unless in frosty weather, when they rustle deliciously under foot, there is a feeling of damp discomfort about them! the leaves of Occidental plane and of American oak shew the most variety of colour : while, the large foliage of polygonum, when withered and scattered about like huge fragments of brown paper, is, I think, downright ugly!

How surely does autumn give a tinge of melancholy to a garden reverie ! and how the feeling grows with age ! But it is not like the ideal sorrowfulness of youth, that dwells so marvellous sweet in our remembrance. It is simply that we listen now to the shortened step of the years to come ; it is only that now, we feel and we know, how for us the days are numbered that will bring back the flowers in their season. Even the lilac bunches of autumn crocus, both double and single, which arise here and there on the bare earth without any green about them do not make much cheer. My pleasant paths are all forlorn ; the singing birds are flown or dead, and unbroken silence reigns in the unleaved thickets they once loved so well. There are no delightful surprises now ; quite plainly and bare of all disguise we see the empty nest in the fork of many a leafless branch ; nests, to discover which in the green June days, we used to peep about and part the leaves or peer into the heart of the yew hedge, so very unsuccessfully !

Never do I remember the pinched and hanging stalks and blackened mouldered ruins of summer, to have made the garden look more drearily disconsolate. Yet even now, in the mournfullest wreck-encumbered borders, straight slender stems appear already full of greenest sap and of 'all the wonder that's to be.' As the saying goes, 'when one door shuts another opens.' And so though a thousand regretful memories cling round the autumn garden, and rise in the heart with the scent of dead and dying leaves, there is no time to dwell on them. Winter's happy working day begins. Now is the time to play all manner of new invented games with flower beds and borders, lawns and shrubberies. The laying out of lines in a garden is not perhaps so easy as might be thought. Your design may look well on paper but when actually cut out in the turf, most likely it will come all wrong; and the clearest head will find too late, that essential details of surroundings have been forgot, or not sufficiently taken into account. The work of remodelling our entrance court has in this way been a lesson. It was so hard to get the curves and angles right, and to make the lines fit in,—chiefly it must be admitted by reason of irregularity in the old walls. A cherry tree, a straggling old apple, and some worn out greengages against the wall all taken away, have made the trimmed pyramid yews look larger; each yew now stands out in solid blackness from his setting of rounded turf. And now lovely clamberers must be chosen for the old brick walls denuded of their fruit trees. There must certainly be blue ceanothus and a passion flower, and above all a scarlet pyracanthus.

I know not what curious thread of far-off association gives this common wall-tree its fascination, at least for myself. I only know the peculiar thrill that invariably startles me whenever I see one covered with ripe fruit. There is a pyracanthus trained up the common wooden paling of a little roadside dwelling that I often have to pass. Familiarity affects not the kind of shock of satisfaction which the sight of its orange red berries never fails to bring.

It is something like, when in music a minor chord drops at once into the full major harmony. So without doubt a pyracanthus must be planted. Only now, in the gloom and damp, we seem to know the full value of scarlet geranium. There are a goodly number of them grown under glass in the frames, and never in the hottest days in August have such scarlet splendours shot from the blossoms. They absolutely flash red rays of burning fire from the glasses on the table. Fireball we find the best for cutting in November. Henri Jacobi is too sombre. Vesuvius is gaiety itself, but Fireball is best. A few starry gold-eyed marguerites, should be mixed in, and there must be no leaves ; the stalks of tender green showing all criss-cross within the clear glass, are relief enough. A glass full of such brilliant colour as this, will illumine the dulness of the gloomiest mid-winter day.

Thus far goes my garden diary of 1887. This 30th of November four years after, is cold and damp and shrouded in a thick white fog. There have been troublous times of wet and wind with alternating frosts. The earth is saturated with moisture : so much so that the very worms are made uncomfortable in it, and wriggle up to the outer air, making tracks across the wet walks where they lie at last all pale and watery, and somewhat unpleasanter than usual.

Change and decay in the garden have gone on the same. The passion flower and the blue ceanothus were planted, bloomed and flourished for a season, and then last winter perished in the frost. The red pyraneanthus planted with them is in its place, all scarlet, and netted from the birds. About the middle of the month a great south wind raged for all one night and day, and our one young American oak fell, snapped close to the root : so there is an end of the rich autumnal foliage which had been a joy each year while it lived with us. A yet greater loss is one of the mighty elms, in the house meadow. It broke right in half, and fell with such violence that big limbs of it dug into the tennis lawn and there stuck fast several feet deep. The tree measured (half of it standing firm and half stretched on the turf), over 120 feet, and all of it fine sound-hearted timber. It must have been soon after that, I went out to enjoy the tremendous music of the storm, raging in the tops of the elms, and watched the old accacia rock and heave up and down from the very roots. It seemed as though every heave might be its last. For on every side but one the roots had entirely given way. It did not altogether go that day. But the poor old accacia tree is sentenced, and before winter ends the axe will have laid it low. Yet one cannot but feel sorry for the nuthatches! no other tree will afford them with such conveniently rough bark, for the cracking of their nuts. Up to last week the garden has been full of roses. Pink and crimson and creamy tea-roses, all sweet as summer, and quite unheeding of the weather. Even York and Lancasters have tried their best to bloom, and made some sickly little flowers, which were picked off the moment they appeared. We have had bowls full of my favourite china roses, both pink and crimson.

NOVEMBER 30TH 1893.—Last summer our roses did well, although some other gardens told a different story. A new long border was cleared and planted with a great many of the best new roses : very choice and wholly uninteresting. For that new border I had been very anxious to procure what some one just returned from New York, described as 'Jack roses.' I was told they were of a fine crimson red and very profuse bloomers. But these turned out to be nothing but the well-known old General Jackminot, which with the usual love for abbreviation in the United States has come to be simply 'Jack.' The disappointment was soon forgotten in the many rose treasures we have since possessed. Socrates, a lovely rose that hated the border is removed to the green-house, where is a healthy Camellia Rose, making vigorous shoots both long and strong. It takes a very large flower pot now; early in March the lovely white single blossoms will begin to open all over it, their fragrance exquisite and unlike to any other rose,—and the perfume seems to live within the centre of its yellow stamens. Then we move out the great pot with its load of loveliness, and it is placed in the shade well sheltered from the wind, to be a joy and delight for full three weeks. This spring, she stood out side by side with a fine pot-plant of Fortune's yellow. The sister roses were both so beautiful one scarce knew which to admire most. I do not think the Camellia Rose (Japan) is often seen in English gardens, but on the Riviera it has long been familiar. At Cannes, the Villa Grand Bois is half covered with it. And in the gardens of La Mortola between Menton and Ventimiglia, memory recalls with delight long lovely garlands of it enwreathing the low thickets of rose and aloe. In the frames we have nearly half a score of charming little shrubby roses grown from Indian seed. The flowers as yet are very small, but highly scented and deep in colour, keeping their rich pink when dried. Lucille, an old-fashioned climber—famous for the charm of its bud—promises well on the wire rose-arches. To these have been lately added the long-desired old Celestial rose and the Jacobite white rose. This last is a gift straight from a garden in the Chanonry, Aberdeen Old Town, where 'it has always been,' as one says. It is the very rose they loved and wore for Prince Charlie. Rosa cinnamomea (the Willow rose), grows most luxuriantly with us, and even threatens to become tiresome. Its flowers are marked by the lovely peculiarity of a little round pink pointal. Yet even as I write, a doubt arises whether after all it *is* really cinnamomea! or whether it be not rather rosa pomefera major, the great Apple Rose of Parkinson. Portions of his description of each would suit in part either of these two roses, while a third 'the rose without thorns,' or the 'marbled rose,' is still more like.

I would not quarrel with my Parkinson; but certainly his descriptions of the roses of his day, are perhaps somewhat involved.

N

Our Willow rose might in these days be thus described :— 'Smooth long stems with infrequent thorns at intervals set singly or in pairs, tufted with narrow willow-shaped leaves in the midst of which appear the flowers, five-petalled, of a full pink colour. In the centre of each flower a little round pink button or pointal surrounded by yellow stamens. The hips are dark red and round like little russet pippins, and these tiny apples being hairy while young, become in time quite smooth and shining.' There exist no doubts, however, about the Velvet rose (Rosa tholoserica simplex et multiplex). A few plants of this neglected rose, survive in our older shrubberies, the flower is neatly made and small : semi-double, of a deep, black-crimson colour, and velvety with yellow threads. The velvet rose is not very good for cutting, as it never lasts. Yet by its so great abundance in the season of its bloom, I am always tempted to gather of it. The Ayrshire rose has been added to our store, but as yet the rooted cuttings have not left their nursery.

In all the garden there are but two
bushes of pink Cabbage rose. The North
seems to greatly favour this old beauty.
All through August last and a part of
September, roadside cottage gardens on
Deeside were ideal, with a perfumed pink
profusion of them. Everywhere rows of
large untidy bushes were seen hung all
over with round and heavy roses. Just
one remnant of a Crested rose (once so
fashionable), survives, I believe, somewhere among the Rhododendrons in the
Boccage. I discovered it by chance two
years ago ; but somehow it slipt away again
before that summer ended, and it has never
since been seen. The little Rose de Meaux
too—joy of our childhood—has disappeared
from the border where once it grew, and
so has the Fairy Rose disappeared from
the kitchen garden. I have heard of little
hedges of the Fairy rose instead of box
edgings. But amongst all the roses of
other days, the Celestial rose is surely
queen ! The little round Burnet Roses,
white and yellow, are sweetest of all.

In the east border, under the wall, two

grand old Baron Prevost, are covered with a second bloom, or rather their bloom has never ceased all summer long. These trees are over six feet in height, having been originally worked on a stem as tree roses. I have known them for upwards of twenty-six years. But the name of the Celestial sets me dreaming of the loveliness of many a half-forgotten rose of our grandmothers' gardens : and musing, appears before me like a dream, an old Scotch garden as I saw it on a July day a year ago—and hope again to see it summer by summer.

It is just an old-fashioned Scotch kitchen garden within a beechwood—full of fine potatoes and turnips and berries, and flower borders. Two acres gently sloping to the south, enclosed within lofty grey granite walls which are almost hidden behind ancient cherry, pear, and apple trees. The granite walls enclose three sides, and the fourth, the south side, is picturesquely fenced, though the fencing may be unpropitious enough for a kitchen garden. A low stone wall with narrow tall brick pillars rising above it at intervals and a woodwork trellis of faded green between each. The trellis is heavily overgrown with great masses of ivy and honeysuckle — white honeysuckle just now in richest bloom and fragrance—and is partly hidden by the wild growth of a neglected shrubbery border where tall white campanula and Aaron's rod, Solomon's seal, and weedy Turk's cap lilies, struggle to the light through a wilderness of guelder rose and spindle, and holly and gean trees.

Pushing open the door, between the heavy granite door posts quite overcanopied with honeysuckle, and with the gooseberry and raspberry and snowberry, that for many a year have seeded and grown up in unheeded luxuriance from every cranny in the stones—the plan of the garden is disclosed at once. It is very simple: a long straight walk between borders of turf and flowers and two hedges of cotoneaster, leading up to a green door at the other end; a walk all round, and four cross walks. After the true old Scotch style, each walk is bordered with flowers and gooseberry and currant bushes, roses and columbines, with a thousand other less familiar plants beside. But the old - fashioned roses are the glory and the charm of the garden. Long before La France was born, or Gloire de Dijon's name was heard, these beautiful gay damasks and York and Lancasters, grew and flourished here. And strange to say, here their old titles also have survived.

Two tall sweet briers guard the entrance of the brier cross-walk. To-day they are *covered* with little pink roses, like nothing I have ever seen since Masaccio's fresco in the Ricardi palace at Florence, where rose-crowned angels kneel in a row beside a low rose hedge. One knows not on which side to look, so splendid on either hand is the array of roses, red and white ; heavy - headed cabbage roses, roses of Provence and pink moss roses in the wildest profusion. The crimson damask are so ' brode ' as old garden-writers say, so vigorous, so replete with colour and with fragrance, they literally glow like

crimson lamps of fire, whenever the sky
is overcast. Broad roses, indeed they are,
for the least of them will measure five
inches across with ten great petals and
smaller ones besides, around the centre
diadem of bright gold stamens, from the
midst of which rises the stiff, thick column
of clustered pistil. It is difficult to see or
smell or to write of these damasks without an enthusiasm that seems to carry
one away! Fine clumps of English iris
vary with their exquisite tints of lilac
or violet and speckled mauve, the all-
prevailing rose-red pink and white. This
iris is far more Scotch than English, for
there is scarce a cottage garden round
about in Aberdeenshire without its iris
clumps. I know a little garden there,
that grows them in a wonderful double
line, milk-white. 'Aye,' responds the
gudewife when the great number of her
white flowers is admired, ' I just slice 'em
like ing'ons (onions) and digs them in.'
And beside the irises, thrives in deep
fiery crimson, a certain double dwarf Sweet
William—the gardener's pride—and the

clear amber-yellow of low-growing œnothera. Here too, is Sauguinaria Canadensis.

A faint scent of bergamot leads you to
a plant or two of purplish Fraxinella.
Pass your hand across the leaves, and the
perfume will cling to it ; or come again
after dark and strike a match under its
nose ! and the flowers will blaze up and
crackle and be none the worse. Purple
Canterbury bells as big as coffee cups with
saucers too, contrast beautifully with the
almost ethereal purity of the great white
Cabbage, or Provence, roses, which toss
themselves in singular confusion of crossing
bud and bloom. I believe this last
came out anew last year as the York rose.
Years ago, it was the Neapolitan rose.
Could she but open her petals more tidily
she would be supreme. Great bushes of it
alternate in another walk with old pink
cabbage and moss roses. The former has
such a heavy head that one needs must
hold it up to look within at the round,
pink, bird's nest. And then it strikes one
at once, that this was the type of the rose
of ancient sculpture—of the Cathedral at

Amiens : and also of Mary Moser's crayons,
and of the once fashionable papier-mâché
tea-trays, and card-board painted hand-
screens, and all the rest of the flower-art of
that period when the century was young.
But now the brier walk leads into the
broad side walk, and here begins the reign
of Velvet roses, sweetest of them all,
though they last for but one brief day or
so. The flower is made of real silk velvet
leaves, full of delicious fragrance, wine-
dark in colour. The learned dispute about
which was the Velvet rose. But the
guardian of this old Scotch garden has no
such doubts; 'This' he says 'is the Velvet
rose.' Just for the pleasure of hearing
them, I like to pretend ignorance, and ask
him for the name of this or that rose.
Quite naturally, and without hesitation he
will answer, 'the Velvet rose,' or 'the
damask,' or 'the white cabbage,' etc., as
if they were the modernest roses !

Here and there the finer pink of a careless, semi-double flower, marks an un-
named variety, nearly allied to the crested
rose. On the shady side of the garden,

among the potatoes, distinguished by its grace of growth, by its bluish-green leaf, and its half single snow-white flower, we know the ancient Jacobite rose. Until I knew its name, it used to seem so strange, that in some parts, never a road-side cottage, or little muirland dwelling, if no more than a 'butt and a ben,' but has its white rose bush growing by the door, or straggling across the dyke. It is the old Jacobite rose, and its presence thus surviving still among us, is a living link with those far off troubled times, when Prince Charlie was the darling of the people, and his rose, the 'rose that's like the sna',' was planted by every house-wall in that north land of loyalty. They had their white rose always near, though they might not dare to wear it. One other forgotten rose of beauty, the oft named Celestial, is recalled by the shapely oval bud of the Jacobite. Every old rose has its special attribute or character. The attribute of this, is an exquisite neatness, combined with the most consummate loveliness. Though impossible to paint it in words, it is like this : — Leaves cold blue-green, evenly serrated. The bud, packed as if by hand (a fairy's hand !) opens slowly, leaf by leaf. The open flower is almost flat, and forms into a perfect circle, suffused with a delicious pink, which is like no other pink. They did well who named it rose of Heaven, for other roses come not near to equal the fairness of it—faultless in its purity of shape and colour.

How few remember now that lovely flower : like many another sweet old thing —it has gone out of fashion. New roses give so little real pleasure ! They are so often without scent ; and is not the fragrance of it, the rose's soul ? But I know little of them, and incline to rank them with exhibition chrysanthemums, which one loathes. Sometimes, however, it is, I confess, love at first sight. It was so when first I saw 'Lady Folkestone'— and the so-called 'white La France.' These two came to live in the garden, and I hope never to lose the charm of their fair beauty. Once in a vision I saw a rose ! I believe it has never bloomed on earth ; but perhaps it may come some happy day among the newly invented briers. It was a single-flowered white rose, the petals delicately edged with pink.

DECEMBER

XIII

DECEMBER

'The steadfast mind that to the end
  Is fortune's victor still,
Hath yet a fear, though Fate befriend,
  A hope though all seem ill.
Jove can at will the winter send,
  Or call the spring at will.'
            William Watson (Odes of Horace).

DECEMBER 24TH.—There are roses, real pink roses, full blown in the garden still. Tea roses also are there, showing large firm buds which look resolved to open. There are little white strawberry blossoms shining among the wild strawberry leaves in the south border under the windows of the house. 'All is seeming, nothing is,' at the season of this nigh two thousand year old anniversary. And thus in the days long gone by, a dream like this I dreamed :—

XIV

ON CHRISTMAS EVE

A Mother's Dream

CHRISTMAS was with us, almost before we were aware, and the Christmas tree had not yet been cut in the Fir wood. Soon it would be carried home to be decked in burning lights and tinsel toys. And the children began to ask, 'Mother, where are we to have the Christmas tree?' and she made answer quietly, 'In the wood, to-night.' But the elder children were displeased; and one said the night was cold, and another said the way was slippery, and none of them would leave the warm fireside. And so the children agreed they would not go out to find the Christmas tree in the dark wood. Only the little one, the boy with the fair round face and the flowing hair—he softly stole his hand into his mother's, and looking up in her eyes, he said, 'I will go with you!' So they went out both of them together into the still starlight. The night was clear and cold and the little one must have his fur hood, and the warm cloak must be closely wrapped round him. And they went down the steps into the garden and so across the lawn through the narrow gate into the wild dark wood. And the child's eyes were full of wonder as he saw the great golden stars above the trees, and knew not they were God's eternal word written in the heavens.

Silently we went on our way. The green moss under our feet, the bare black stems of ancient forest trees rising up on either hand, till we came where two paths crossed, and there, at the entering in of the wood where the fir trees began—stood three Angels. They were clad in moon-white raiment, and crowned with roses, pure roses of Paradise, whose far off fragrance stirred our very heart.

The countenance of the angels was but dimly seen, by reason of a dazzling glory round their heads—yet, it seemed as though they smiled, and beckoned to us with the hand. A gentle wind arose and swayed

o

the branches over head—and there was the sound of murmurous music amid the pines. And deeper and further into the deep wood the child and I passed onward, silently hand in hand, and many fair trees we passed by, but found not the tree we sought. And about the middle of the way, the three angels parted from us, and afar off shone a beautiful light, and it seemed to me that we saw very nigh the light of the Christmas tree! But as we drew more near, behold it was not the tree but a bright star shining low in the wood. And now I knew not any longer where we were, for the trees were about us no more, but only a wide moonlit mountain land.

Cold moonbeams whitened the flocks upon a thousand hills, and the Star had paled its light in the glory streaming forth from the open door of a lowly ruined hut beneath it. The radiance grew and grew until there was not any more night. And then, with our eyes we beheld the Virgin Mother; and her Holy Child lay beside her in the manger; and the ox and the ass were there. The shepherds also were kneeling at His feet.

Then we two in the outer blackness drew very near and trembled. And filled with joy, and with rapturous awe, we knelt with the shepherds of Bethlehem, and we gazed at the babe through tears of love and holy fear. And while we gazed, a note of utter sweetness rose and swelled until it became like the solemn sound of an organ, until it filled all the place where we were, and shook the walls of the lowly cattle shed bursting and shattering up through the roof. And there was a rushing sound as of innumerable multitudes of angels' wings, and they were like sharp-pointed flames of fire thronging all around and upward. In our ears we heard pealing and echoing, and dying away amidst the hills, the words of the ancient song of Peace, 'Glory to God, and Peace on earth.' We hid our faces in our hands, and so the vision departed from our sight, and the fir trees closed in once more around us. So dreamfully we wandered on, the child's face all glowing yet, and bright with the shining of the heavenly light that we had seen, his cheek still wet with happy tears.

Low in the valley where in spring we found the subtle-scented primroses, and where snow-drops make soft moonlight under the trees in early days of March, there, in an open space at last we saw the Christmas Tree.

Alone under the starry sky the Tree burnt with a great glow of golden fruits amid the living fire of myriads of precious stones, all glorious from the lowest to the topmost branch, making in that shady place so great a splendour that we could see the little birds with their heads turned under their wing-feathers, sleeping in the winter trees. The light awoke them not, but round the trees soft wild furry creatures, with merry, jet-black eyes, peeped here and there. And here and there crept from underneath some stone or withered leaf, the slow toad, with a glittering jewel in her head. In and out amongst the shining lights played little flashes of emerald green.

Strange wonder with a delicious surprise
held the child's lips that he could not
speak. And the mother gently led him
by the hand up to the beauteous tree, and
pointing to the ripe living fruits that hung
thereon, she whispered : ' They are yours ! '
They were of such kinds as ripen not in
earthly gardens. The radiance and the
colours of them shone from a heavenly
land, where grow unchecked the fruits of
love and joy and peace, of wisdom and of
eternal life and innocence. Wreathed
about the branches were garlands of the
freshest flowers, pure flowers of meekness
and gentleness and long-suffering and truth.
And amidst of these immortal flowers and
fruit, half hidden by their bloom, far far up
beyond our reach, hung many crowns of
divers kinds—jewelled crowns of delight,
and rainbow crowns of fancy, white cold
snow-crowns, and royal crowns of fire, and
pale crowns of fear—and silvery chains
festooned with pearls which are tears . . .
But on all these we set not our eyes. For
near the very summit of the green pyramid
of glory, hung one beautiful flower-crown—

rose-hued and fire-hearted even in that clear midnight, the Crown of Love outshone the very stars in heaven. And I cried, 'Oh my little one, let us reach down to us the Crown of Love.' And then they stretched out their arms, though the love-crown hung so far above. . . . And suddenly the sky was overcast and heavy clouds hid all the stars. And a shuddering blast swept past through the wood spreading wide the child's long hair . . . . and the fair fruits and the garlands fell from the Christmas Tree, and the rose leaves were blown away and scattered, and the place was filled with a wild storm of sweetness.

One only diadem remained, while all the rest had faded, even as an evening mist shimmering through the ruined roses; and the wind shook the trees, so that the Love-crown floated down to us. But even then as with eager hand we seemed to grasp them, the flowers were not; but the thorns of the Crown of Pain pierced through the mother's heart as she clasped it close, and the rose leaves became drops of blood. Then I turned in anguish to my child. But he had folded his hands unhurt upon his breast, and gazed smiling, with joyful eyes upon those sharp naked thorns. And she knew that the little one perceived only the Divine and pearly radiance, which for her, shone as a dim halo of tears around the crimsoned wreath . . . . Gathered in her arms the mother held the child for a moment, there, in the dewy twilight of a green Christmas dawn : while far-heard Christmas bells awoke the day to love and holy joy. And the night had departed like a by-gone dream. And there, with tender-taken breath slept my little one beside me, and a pure white rose-bud lay upon the pillow. At the window a robin sang a short, sweet carol to the breaking day.

XV

CHRISTMAS DAY

EX UMBRA *

'IN twilight while I walk alone
    A strange voice calls me, clear and low ;
A shadowy hand that seeks my own,
    Cold as the wind and soft as snow,
Still leads me, leads me as I pass
    Across the grey December grass.

'The village windows beckon still
    With glow of amber and of gold ;
But my way lies along the hill,
    My road must cross the frosty wold ;
And still I feel and still I see
    The darkness round me deep and free.'

IN the dark, clear, early morning, the thrushes are singing with soft under voices. At this early hour before sunrise they are not afraid, and many a dear speckled breast and swelling throat is plainly to be seen in the elms and limes, on branches overhanging the road.

* By permission of Editor *Pall Mall Gazette.*

A white Christmas is beautiful, but I think I like almost better the soft warm grey which the wild birds love. There is a feeling that underneath the dim grass comes then a stirring of life: that the snowdrops and crocuses are feeling upwards and are ready to break through to the light.

Poor birds! Poor little flowers! It is all a dream, and the worst of winter is to come: soon or late it has to be, and January will have no pity.

What would life be without Hope? How should we endure the melancholy of the Iris ground at this moment, covered as it is with apparently decaying roots and broken rubbish of wet, dead leaves, did not the mind's eye see it in its glow of summer bloom, as we hope to see it a few months hence! Beside the narrow aqueduct that runs down to us from the village ponds a mile distant (and which is always dry except in winter when it is not wanted) a plantation of Japanese iris Kœmpferi has been made :—that is, they were meant to be the Japanese, but when they arrived

from Holland they turned out to be mostly
another sort, with narrow leaves and
smaller flowers. Nevertheless they are
very charming with their varieties of pure
white and lilac and purple, and some of the
white have broad petals, although their
leaves are narrow. The place is too dry
for them to succeed perfectly : the Kœmpferi should grow close to the water, by a
lake or a stream. I have laboured hard
for them, however, collecting stones and
wheeling them (in an old perambu-
lator) and planting them about the roots
to keep whatever moisture there may
be.

In stones, I have the greatest faith. I
like to arrange them with my own hands,
round the roots I love the most. It may
be fancy, but yet a pleasant fancy dashed
with truth, that many a lovely favourite
has been thus saved from withering death.
The moss-roses love these stones ! So
does a curious red-brown iris which made no
flowers for three years after being transplanted from its own old home in the West.
Yet there are several plants who refuse to

be comforted, or to believe that the stones I
give to them are bread! Iris Susiana—
grand, melancholy, bizarre, half-mourning
iris!—once flowered magnificently in the
garden. But that was five or six years ago.
Since then, excepting in the greenhouse,
she has shown no sign of any wish to bloom.
No careful choice of situation, no sheltering
with glass during October and November
has yet availed to move her rigid self-
reserve. Ground up lime-stone mixed
well with the soil might be a help. The
strong mixture of granite in the soil of
Scotch gardens may be perhaps the secret
of the vigour and strength of colour and
larger size of their flowers, compared with
ours. In Riviera gardens, the black iris
luxuriates. Long ago in one of these
gardens by the sea, groups of it in full
flower grew on the green margin of a little
pool of water. Half hidden among the
great leaves stood a low stone sun-dial,
whose motto round about it went thus:
'Vado e vengo, ogni giorno, ma tu andrai
senza ritorno.' The music of the words
still seems to haunt the soul in opal

tinted dreams, whose colour somehow
does not fade with the fading light of
other days.

Snowflake from the Thames